DATE DUE

JUN 24 1980	JY 8 '86	[illegible]
MAY 9 1981	AG 1 '86	[illegible] 02
JUN 6 1981	JY 6 '87	AP 22 '04
JUN 25 1981	JE 28 '91	MR 27 '06
JUL 21 1981	JY 20 '92	OC 14 '14
AUG 18 1981	MAY 04 '93	JE 30 '15
AUG. 2 1982	JUN 01 '95	[illegible] 19 '18
NOV. 24 1982	DEC 04 '96	JY 30 '19
JUL. 29 1983	AUG 08 '97	
APR. 2 1984	MAR 04 '98	
JUN. 29 1984	MAR 17 '98	
DEC. 22 1984	JUL 06 '98	
MAR. 20 1985	JUL 27 '98	
MY 18 '85	SEP 02 '98	
JUN. 14 1985	AP 12 '99	

Haywood, Carolyn
Betsy's busy summer

BETSY'S BUSY SUMMER

By the Same Author

Published by William Morrow and Company

EDDIE MAKES MUSIC. 1957

BETSY'S BUSY SUMMER. 1956

EDDIE AND HIS BIG DEALS. 1955

BETSY AND THE CIRCUS. 1954

EDDIE'S PAY DIRT. 1953

THE MIXED-UP TWINS. 1952

EDDIE AND GARDENIA. 1951

BETSY'S LITTLE STAR. 1950

EDDIE AND THE FIRE ENGINE. 1949

PENNY GOES TO CAMP. 1948

LITTLE EDDIE. 1947

Published by Harcourt, Brace and Company

PENNY AND PETER. 1946

BETSY AND THE BOYS. 1945

HERE'S A PENNY. 1944

BACK TO SCHOOL WITH BETSY. 1943

PRIMROSE DAY. 1942

BETSY AND BILLY. 1941

TWO AND TWO ARE FOUR. 1940

"B" IS FOR BETSY. 1939

BETSY'S BUSY SUMMER

Written and Illustrated by
CAROLYN HAYWOOD

WILLIAM MORROW & COMPANY, *New York, 1956*

One chapter of this book has appeared as a story in *Jack and Jill* magazine.

FOURTH PRINTING, JUNE, 1958

Published simultaneously in the Dominion of Canada by George J. McLeod Limited, Toronto.

Printed in the United States of America.

Library of Congress Catalog Card Number: 56-7894

To the Librarians,
past and present,
of the Free Library of Philadelphia
who have helped and encouraged me.

CONTENTS

BETSY'S BUSY SUMMER

CHAPTER 1

THE DUCKESS AND THE GOLDFISH

THE hot weather began the week before school closed. The children wriggled in their seats, fanned themselves with sheets of yellow paper, put their heads down on their desks, and complained that it was too hot to go to school. There was always some-one at the drinking fountain, and the girls wet their handkerchiefs and wiped their faces. The only time the children did not mind the heat was at recess time. Then they ran and jumped and climbed and swung, just as though it were winter.

By the time school closed in the last week in June, everyone had decided that the hot weather had come to stay. All the fathers and mothers still complained about the heat, but never the children. Now that they did not have to go to school, they didn't seem to know that it was hot. The air was filled with their shouts as they raced and ran and played.

There was almost always a crowd of them playing in Betsy's yard. Betsy had a big yard to play in. It was all around the house, but the biggest part was in the back, where Betsy's mother had a garden. A path ran through the garden to the far end, where Betsy's father had made a pool. It was not very big and it was not very deep, but the eight goldfish that lived in it seemed to find it a pleasant place. At the end of Betsy's yard a stone wall ran between it and the Jacksons' place.

Betsy had always liked the big yard, but this summer t was nicer than ever, because there was a summerhouse in it. As long as Betsy could remember, her father had told her about the summerhouse that had been in his grandfather's garden. He had played in it when he was a little boy. He had told Betsy and Star many stories about the things that he had done in the summerhouse, and they had often coaxed him to build one for them.

"Oh, they are such old-fashioned things," Father always said. "Nobody builds summerhouses any more. All the neighbors would laugh if I built a summerhouse in the yard." But this spring he had finally built one. He had spent his Saturdays sawing and hammering, and finally painting the little house all white. It looked like a large bird cage, but the neighbors didn't laugh when it was finished. Instead, they all said to their children, "Why don't you go over to Betsy's and play in the summerhouse?"

It was soon very noticeable that Betsy's summerhouse was going to be the favorite spot for all the neighborhood children during their summer vacation. It was shaded by the trees, and Betsy's father had fastened a big old-fashioned electric fan in the center of the ceiling. It twirled away by the hour, sending a cooling breeze down on the heads of the children when they played there.

One warm day, Betsy and her best friend Ellen were sitting in the summerhouse, sewing new dresses for their dolls. Betsy was making her doll a plaid school dress, and Ellen was making hers a party dress of pink silk.

Betsy's mother had taken the car and gone to market. Betsy's little sister Star and Ellen's little sister Linda were in the garden, playing dress-up ladies. Star was wearing an old housecoat of her mother's. It was pale blue with pink roses. It wrapped around her six times and was held on by a wide sash tied in a large bow in the back. She looked like a little sausage.

Linda had on a black satin dress that had once be-

longed to Star's grandmother. It was held on and held up with many safety pins. Underneath the dress she had on a pink-and-white-checked sun suit. The whole back of the tight little pants was covered with rows of ruffles, which gave the black satin dress a bustle in the rear. The dress had a fishtail train, which Linda swished as she walked up and down the garden path. She was also wearing a black lace scarf over her head.

"I'm a Duckess," said Linda to Star, as she stopped in the walk beside the pool.

"What's a Duckess?" asked Star, who was younger than Linda and didn't know as much.

"Goodness!" said Linda. "Don't you know what a Duckess is?"

Star shook her head.

"Well," said Linda, "a Duckess lives in a castle and she's very, very rich. 'Course, she always has beautiful dresses and she never does anything for herself. Not anything. She never has to put her toys away or . . ." Linda thought for a moment. Then she said, "Or even clean her teeth."

"Oh," said Star, "she would have to clean her teeth. If she didn't clean her teeth, they would all fall out. Not all at once, but one at a time they would."

Linda looked at Star and shook her head. "No, Duckesses are different," she said. Then, with a sweep of her arm, she added, "A Duckess just hands her teeth to a slave and says, 'Here, slave, clean my teeth!' " Linda stuck her chin in the air, kicked her train, and said, "I'm a Duckess, I am." But her foot got caught in her train and she tripped and toppled over. When she tried to get up, she turned the wrong way and rolled right into the pool with the goldfish.

Star screamed, and Betsy and Ellen came running from the summerhouse. They both went down on their knees and pulled Linda to her feet. She was crying very hard and, of course, she was soaking wet. Her black satin dress was blacker and shinier than ever, and the black lace scarf was all over her face, so

that she looked as though she were covered with a lot of black seaweed.

"Don't cry, Linda," said Ellen. "Don't cry. You didn't hurt yourself, did you?"

"I don't know," yelled Linda.

"Did she hurt the fishes?" asked Star. "I hope she didn't hurt our fishes."

"Climb out, Linda," said Ellen, taking hold of Linda's arm. "I'll help you."

Linda made a feeble effort to climb out. Then she said, "I can't."

"Of course you can," said Ellen. "You're not trying."

"I am too," said Linda. "It's too scratchy around the pool."

"Here!" said Betsy, taking hold of Linda's other arm. "We'll pull you up."

"No!" Linda screamed. "You'll scratch me."

"Well, you can't stand there forever," Ellen told her.

"I'll go get the little stepladder out of the kitchen," said Betsy, and she ran off to the house. In a few minutes she came out of the back door with the little stepladder and carried it to the side of the pool.

"Betsy," said Star, who was kneeling beside the pool, "count the fishes. See if she hurt the fishes."

"You can count to eight, Star," said Betsy. "I'm busy. We have to get Linda out." Betsy put the ladder down into the pool. "Now, Linda," she said, "you can climb out."

Star was busy counting the fish. She pointed with her finger as she counted. "One, two, three, four, five, six, seven, eight." Then she said, "She didn't hurt them. They're all there, Betsy. The eight fishes are all there."

"That's good," said Betsy. "Come along, Linda. It's easy now."

Linda had stopped crying. She put her hands on the top step of the ladder and her foot on the lowest step. Betsy and Ellen each took hold of one of her arms.

"I can do it," Linda cried. "I can do it myself." She began to cry again.

"All right!" said Ellen, letting go of her arm. Betsy let go too. Right away, Linda sank back in the water and sat down on the bottom of the pool. The water came up to her neck.

"Linda!" Ellen shouted.

Linda looked up through the drapery of black seaweed. "I like it here," she said. "It's nice in the pool. Nice and cool."

"But it isn't a bathing pool," said Betsy. "It's a fish-pool. Now you've scared the fish twice."

"Linda, you come out of there right away," said Ellen, "or I'll never bring you to play at Betsy's house again."

Linda got up at once and climbed out of the pool. She stood dripping water from her clothes, and a large puddle began to form around her. She looked like a little black seal.

Star was on her knees again, counting the fish.

"One, two, three, four, five, six, seven . . . seven . . . seven," she said. Then she cried out, "Betsy! There are only seven! One of the fishes is gone!"

"You must have counted wrong," said Betsy, and she knelt down beside the pool. She counted the fish. Seven! She counted them again. Seven!

"There were eight when Linda sat down," said Star. "I know there were eight."

Betsy peered into the water. "I don't see the gold one with the black stripes," she said.

"No," said Star. "I don't see it either."

Ellen was busy taking the safety pins out of Linda's clothes. They were hard to take out of the wet satin. Each one came out with a little squeaky sound when she pulled it through the silk. At last Linda stood in her wet sun suit, and the black satin dress lay in a wet heap on the path. The ruffles on the back of her sun suit no longer stuck out.

Suddenly Linda jumped. Then she let out a scream. "Oh! Oh!" she cried. She began hopping up and down, first on one foot and then on the other. "Oh! Oh!" she yelled.

Betsy and Star stopped counting the fish, and Ellen cried, "What's the matter? What's the matter?"

Linda was now running around in circles, stopping every once in a while to dance up and down. "Something's inside! Something's inside!" she screamed.

"Inside where?" Ellen cried.

"Inside my suit! Inside my pants!" cried Linda.

Ellen ran after Linda. "Stand still and I'll get it out." said Ellen.

"It's the fish!" cried Betsy. "I bet it's the fish!"

Just then, Star saw her mother drive into the garage. Star scrambled to her feet and ran to the garage, calling out, "Mother! Mother! Linda's got a fish in her pants! She's got one of our fish in her pants!" Star's mother came hurrying toward the children. By this time Ellen had her hand down the back of Linda's sun suit, but Linda was still hopping up and down.

"Stand still! Stand still!" Ellen kept saying.

Just as Betsy's mother reached them, Ellen pulled out the fish. "Here it is!" she said, handing it over to Betsy.

Betsy looked at the fish. It was still wiggling and its tiny mouth was gaping. She leaned over the pool and dropped it into the water. The four children knelt down to watch it. They were all glad to see it swim off. Betsy looked up at her mother. "Oh, Mother!" she said. "Linda fell into the pool!"

"She looks as though she had," said Mother, looking down at Linda, who was still dripping water from her hair and from her ruffles. She held out her hand to Linda. "Come along with me, dear," she said. "I'll see if I can find something for you to wear that is not too big and not too little."

Linda took hold of Betsy's mother's hand and they walked toward the house. "How did it happen?" Mother asked.

"I was playing I was a Duckess," said Linda.

"I see," said Mother, "and because you were being a duck, you had to go in the water?"

"No! No!" said Linda. "Not a duck, a Duckess. A Duckess lives in a castle and she has slaves to clean her teeth."

"Oh," said Betsy's mother, "and I suppose the slave threw them into the fish pond?"

"No," said Linda. "We weren't playing that." Then she looked up and said, "But that would be a good game, wouldn't it?"

CHAPTER 2

HOW TO MAKE LEMONADE

IT WAS a hot July day. Billy Porter, one of Betsy's friends from school, had come to spend the afternoon with Betsy. "What do you want to do?" Betsy had asked, when Billy arrived.

"I don't know," said Billy. "What do *you* want to do?"

"We could play checkers in the summerhouse," said Betsy.

"We played checkers the last time I came," replied Billy. "Let's do something different. Couldn't we make something?"

"Like what?" said Betsy.

"Fudge," said Billy.

"You mean cook?" said Betsy.

"Yes," said Billy. "I like to cook." He smacked his lips. "I like to eat."

"I can't cook," said Star. "I'm too little."

"Well, you're big enough to eat," said Billy, "and fudge is good."

"Let's ask Mother," said Betsy.

The three children ran into the house. "Mother!" Betsy called. "Mother!"

"I'm talking on the telephone," her mother called back from the front hall.

"Oh! Excuse me, Mother," said Betsy. "Can we make some fudge?"

Mother turned away from the telephone. "Not to-day," she said. "It's too hot. Make some lemonade."

"Oh, good!" said Betsy. "How many lemons shall we use?"

"Two," said her mother, and turned back to the telephone.

"How much water?" said Betsy.

Mother turned to her again. "The pitcher full," she said.

The children ran back to the kitchen. Betsy opened the refrigerator door and took out two lemons. "Here, Billy," she said, "you can squeeze the lemons."

"They have to be rolled first," said Billy. "That makes them soft and juicy."

"I want to roll them," said Star. "I can roll them."

"Let her roll them, Billy," said Betsy.

"Well, I'll show you a good way," said Billy. "Look, you put the lemon on the floor and do it with your foot!" He put the two lemons on the floor and began rolling one of them under his foot. Star watched him for a moment and then she put her foot on the other lemon.

"Mine's getting nice and soft," said Billy.

"It will be nice and dirty," said Betsy.

"I'll wash it," said Billy. "It's almost ready." And then *Pop!* The lemon burst. The juice and seeds flew out on the clean kitchen floor. "Oops!" said Billy, looking down at the mess.

"Now look!" said Betsy. "Billy, you always make a mess of things."

"No, I don't," said Billy. "It was just an accident. I'll wipe it up."

Betsy stooped down and picked up the other lemon that Star had been rolling. "Now we only have one lemon," she said.

"Where's a rag?" Billy asked.

Betsy ran into the hall. Her mother was still talking on the telephone.

Betsy tapped her on the shoulder, and Mother looked up.

"Where's a rag?" Betsy whispered.

"What for?" asked her mother.

"To wipe up the floor," Betsy said. "Billy made a mess with the lemon."

"In the closet under the sink," said her mother.

Betsy found the rag and gave it to Billy. While he cleaned up the floor, Betsy squeezed the remaining lemon and poured the juice into the pitcher. "This won't be very good lemonade," she said, filling the pitcher with water.

Billy flung the rag into the sink. "Aren't there any more lemons?" he asked.

"I didn't see any more," Betsy replied. "You look in the refrigerator."

Billy opened the refrigerator door. He looked on all the shelves and in the storage bins. "I don't see any," he said, "but here's some prune juice. Maybe it would be good with some prune juice."

Betsy ran back to the hall. She waved her hand at her mother, who was still busily talking, and caught her eye. "Now what?" said Mother.

"May we have some prune juice?" Betsy asked.

"Yes, yes," said her mother.

Betsy ran back to the kitchen. "We can have it," she said to Billy.

Billy brought out the prune juice. He poured it into the pitcher until the pitcher was full. Betsy stirred it and then tasted it. "It tastes awful," she said.

"Well, here's a big jar of raspberry jam," said Billy. "Bet that would make it good."

Betsy ran to her mother again. This time she waved both hands. "Mother! Mother!" she said.

Her mother took the receiver from her ear again. "What is it, Betsy?"

"May we have some raspberry jam?"

"Yes," said her mother.

"O.K.," said Betsy, returning to the kitchen. "Bring the jar," she said to Billy.

Billy picked up the big jar of jam. It was very cold, and the warm air of the kitchen made drops of water form on it. It was very slippery. Billy decided to carry it with both hands. He landed it safely on the table.

"Take the lid off," said Betsy.

Billy tried to unscrew it. "It's tight," he said. "You try." Betsy tried with all her strength, but the lid wouldn't budge. "Take it to Mother," she said. "She can get it off."

Billy carried the jar into the hall, holding it tight against his chest with both hands. He stood in front of Betsy's mother at the telephone. He bumped his chin on the lid of the jar and shook his head. Betsy's mother went right on talking. He bumped his chin on the lid again and shook his head.

Betsy's mother removed the receiver from her ear. "Whatever do you want, Billy?"

"Can't get the lid off," replied Billy.

Betsy's mother put the receiver down and took the jar in her hands. She gave the lid a twist and off it came. Then she set the lid back, loosely.

"Thanks," said Billy, and started back to the kitchen. As he crossed the dining room, Star opened the back door to let Thumpy, the cocker spaniel, in. Billy and

Thumpy reached the open door from the dining room into the kitchen at the same moment. Neither one waited for the other to go through, and as Billy was much bigger than Thumpy, he tripped over him. Billy stumbled into the kitchen, and went right on stumbling until he crashed into the screen on the back door. But the door was locked, so there he stopped. The jar of jam was still clutched in his arms like a football, but the lid had flown off during his journey across the kitchen. To Star's great surprise it landed right on top of her head. There it sat like a round hat. Raspberry jam trickled down her forehead.

Billy recovered his balance. He put the jar on the table with a sigh and said, "I'll bet you thought I was going to drop it."

"It's a good thing you didn't," said Betsy, as she spooned up some jam.

"Wait a minute!" Billy cried out. "Haven't you got any sense? That pitcher is going to spill over if you put that much jam in."

Billy looked around the kitchen. "Here!" he said, picking up a brand-new plastic bucket that Betsy's mother had bought the day before. "Let's pour it into this." Betsy emptied the pitcher into the bucket. Suddenly Billy's face brightened. "Say, Betsy!" he said. "Why don't we have a lemonade stand and sell this lemonade? Bet we could make some money, and it would be fun."

"In the summerhouse?" said Betsy.

"No, we'd have to sell it out front," said Billy. "Bet cars would stop. Hot day like this, everybody is thirsty."

"Oh, Billy, let's!" said Betsy, stirring more raspberry jam into the bucket. Then she tasted it again.

"Let me taste it," said Billy.

Betsy washed off the spoon, and Billy tasted the mixture. "Not very good, is it?" said Betsy.

"Just needs sugar," said Billy. "Lots of sugar, and it will be dandy. Where's the sugar?" Billy ran to the closet and opened the door.

"I'll get it," cried Betsy. "I'll get it." Betsy pushed Billy aside and picked up the can marked *Sugar*.

"What's the matter with you, Betsy?" Billy exclaimed. "You act as if I couldn't carry a can of sugar!"

Betsy added sugar to the bucket, while Billy brought ice cubes from the refrigerator and dropped them into the pail one by one. "You know what, Betsy?" he said. "This was a wonderful idea. We'll make money sure."

Betsy looked inside the can of sugar. "There isn't very much sugar left," she said, and emptied the can into the lemonade.

Each of the children tasted the drink again. "It's not sweet enough," said Billy. "It doesn't taste like anything."

"Well, there isn't any more sugar," said Betsy.

Billy opened the closet door and looked on the shelves. "Here's some molasses," he said. "That's sweet."

Betsy lifted down the jar of molasses and poured some of it into the bucket. "Now let's try it," she said.

After several tastes, they both agreed that the drink was sweet enough, and Billy went off to the garage to get a wooden box to use as a table.

All this time, Star was sitting on the back step, licking jam off the jam lid. There was not only jam on her forehead. There was jam all over her little button of a nose and on her chin, and there were spots down the front of her dress. She looked as though she had been through a battle. Now she came into the house and put the jam lid down on the sink. She had licked it clean. She went through the dining room and into the front hall.

Betsy picked up a soup ladle in one hand and the bucket in the other. As she carried them out the kitchen door, she heard her mother cry out, "Oh, Star's cut her head! I'll have to hang up. Good-by, good-by! The child is covered with blood!"

Betsy went right on out to the street with the bucket. She knew that her mother would soon find out that Star was covered with jam.

CHAPTER 3
FOR SALE—LEMONADE

BILLY placed the wooden box on the sidewalk right beside the curb. "See!" he said. "Cars can stop right here. We'll give 'em curb service."

Betsy lifted the bucket up on the box. "Get two chairs out of the summerhouse," she said. "I'll get some glasses."

They both ran off but were soon back by the stand. "We have to have a sign," said Billy. "Have to tack it on the box."

"Oh, yes!" said Betsy, and she went to get a piece of paper. She found a large piece of white wrapping paper and picked out a bright green crayon from her crayon box. Then she went back to Billy. "What do you think we should call it?" she asked, as she spread the paper out on the box beside the bucket.

"Why, lemonade," Billy answered.

"But it doesn't look like lemonade," said Betsy.

Billy looked into the bucket. "Well, call it raspberryade," he said. "It looks like raspberryade. You can see seeds floating around."

"I don't know how to spell raspberryade," said Betsy. "Do you know how to spell it?"

"Sure," said Billy.

"Well, how?" Betsy made a big green ***R*** on the paper.

"Uh," said Billy, "well, maybe we better call it pruneade."

"But I've made an ***R,***" said Betsy.

"Put a ***P*** in front of it," Billy suggested.

Betsy laid down her crayon. "Nobody is going to

stop and buy pruneade," she said. "Nobody ever heard of it."

"Well, call it lemonade," said Billy. "Everybody will stop if it says lemonade."

"I told you I have an *R* on the paper," said Betsy. "And there isn't any *R* in lemonade. You said you knew how to spell raspberryade. Go ahead and spell it."

"O.K., O.K.," said Billy. "But I don't think we'll be able to sell it if we call it raspberryade."

"Yes, we will," Betsy insisted. "Go ahead and spell it."

"O.K.," said Billy. "R-a-z-b-u-r-y-a-i-d."

"Slowly," said Betsy.

Billy spelled it out again slowly, and Betsy carefully made the letters. "Are you sure that's right?" she asked, when she had finished.

Billy looked over Betsy's shoulder. "Looks right to me," he said. Then he added, "Maybe it needs an *E* on the end. An awful lot of words have *E* on the end. Better put an *E* on the end."

FOR SALE—LEMONADE

Betsy added an *E* and underneath the word she wrote, *5 Cents a Glass*. Then she said, "Have you any thumbtacks, Billy?" Billy went through his pockets and came up with three thumbtacks. He fastened the sign to the front of the wooden box. Then the two children sat down to wait for customers. They watched each car as it drove toward them, and looked disappointed as it drove by without stopping. After a while they each drank a glass of raspberryade to cheer themselves up. The ice had melted, but it was still cold.

"It's terribly sweet," said Betsy. "I don't think we should have put the molasses in it."

"Nothing can be too sweet," said Billy. "I think it's super."

Finally a car stopped. Two men were in the front seat. "Just what I want," said the driver, "a good cold drink. Fill up two glasses. The biggest ones you have there."

"Here's a quarter," said the other man, handing a coin to Billy. "Keep the change."

"Thanks!" said Billy, his face beaming.

Betsy dipped up the raspberryade and poured it into a glass. The drink showed through the glass. It was not exactly brown and it was not exactly lavender and you couldn't say that it was exactly gray. It was a mixture of all three colors.

The men in the car looked surprised when Billy handed them the glasses. The man at the wheel looked at his glass and then he looked at the children. They were busy admiring the quarter, so he quietly emptied the glass out of the window of the car. Then he took the glass from the other man's hand and poured it out of the window, too.

"Hope it won't take the paint off the car," said his companion. Then he handed the empty glasses to Billy. "Did you like it?" Billy asked.

"Remarkable stuff," said the man. "Too bad you haven't any ice cream to put in it."

"So long!" the driver called out, as he started the car. "Wish you luck."

"Good-by," the children called back. "Thanks!"

"Now we're making money," said Billy.

He and Betsy sat beside their stand all afternoon, but no more cars stopped. Several people walking by stopped and looked into the bucket, but they didn't buy any raspberryade. Finally Billy said to Betsy, "Do you want another glass, Betsy?"

"I don't think so," Betsy answered.

"Don't you like it?" Billy asked.

"Oh, sure I like it," said Betsy. "*You* have some more."

Billy looked into the bucket. "No, I don't think I want any more," he said.

After a while Betsy's mother called from the front window, "Billy, I'm going to take you home in about ten minutes."

"Oh, dear!" said Betsy. "We haven't sold very much."

"Well, no," said Billy, "but we each have a half of a quarter."

"That's twelve and a half cents each," said Betsy, who was much better in arithmetic than in spelling.

"That's right," said Billy.

"How are we going to divide it?" Betsy asked.

"Well, you take twelve cents and I'll take twelve cents and we'll buy one cent's worth of jelly beans and divide 'em between us," said Billy.

"But you get thirteen jelly beans for a penny," said Betsy. "That would be six and a half jelly beans apiece."

"Well, what's the matter with that? You can cut a jelly bean in half."

"I tell you what," said Betsy. "Let's give the penny to Star. Then she'll feel that she earned something."

"But she didn't do anything," Billy protested. "She just licked the jam off the lid."

"Let's give it to her anyway," said Betsy.

"O.K.," said Billy.

Just at that moment, the only horse and wagon in the town came around the corner. It was the parcel-post wagon. When Billy saw it he called out, "Here comes

RAZBURYAIDE
5 CENTS A GLASS

Dolly and Mr. Fisher!" All the children knew Dolly, the horse. She was a gentle old horse with a white star between her kind eyes. "Oh, let's give some raspberryade to Mr. Fisher," Billy added.

"Yes, let's," said Betsy. "We'll give it to him for nothing, because he's so nice."

Dolly came toward them. *Clop! Clop! Clop!*

"Hello, Mr. Fisher!" Billy called out.

"Hello!" Mr. Fisher replied. He drew up beside the stand. "What's this?" he asked.

"It's raspberryade," said Betsy, "and we want to give you some."

"You don't have to pay anything, Mr. Fisher," said Billy. "We want to give it to you free."

Mr. Fisher jumped down. He looked into the bucket. "Oh, thanks," he said, "thanks. That's very kind of you, but I couldn't drink a thing. Just couldn't drink a thing." Then when he saw the disappointment on the children's faces, he said, "Had watermelon for my lunch. Filled me up."

"Oh, that's too bad," said Billy.

"Maybe Dolly would like some," Betsy suggested hopefully.

"I'll bet she would," Billy cried. "Here, Mr. Fisher, give her the bucket. We have to shut up shop now, anyway."

Billy handed the bucket to Mr. Fisher, who held it under Dolly's nose. She put her head into the bucket and sucked up some of the raspberryade. Then she lifted her head and let out a long neigh.

"She likes it, doesn't she?" said Billy.

But Dolly wouldn't come back for more. She shook her head, and Mr. Fisher thought that Dolly's eyes did not look as kind as they usually did. "Guess she's had enough," he said, and he handed the bucket back to Billy. Dolly clopped off down the street, while Mr. Fisher delivered a parcel next door.

"Well," said Billy, "guess we might as well put the rest on the flower bed."

"Guess so," said Betsy.

Billy emptied the bucket on the flower bed. "Maybe raspberries will come up," he said hopefully.

Betsy laughed. "Or prunes," she added.

Star came out the front door. She had a clean face and a clean dress and her hair was still wet, because her mother had washed it. "Betsy," she said, "I didn't have any lemonade at all. Where's the lemonade?"

"We just watered the flowers with it," said Billy. "But we're going to give you a penny."

"Oh!" said Star. "Where is it?"

"In this quarter," said Billy. "I'll ask your mother to change it. Then you can have the penny."

The three children walked, one behind the other, to the back of the house. Billy carried the wooden box. Betsy carried the bucket, filled with empty glasses, and Star carried the ladle.

The sign *Razburyaide, 5 Cents a Glass* blew down the street, and Betsy's father picked it up as he came home from the office. "Whee!" he said. "I'll bet that was a knockout drink!"

CHAPTER 4

"YOU HAVE TO HAVE BACON GREASE"

BETSY and Billy and Ellen were sitting in the summerhouse one morning, each one busy with big sheets of paper and a box of water colors. Betsy had fastened her paper to a board, which she rested against the back of a chair. Billy was lying flat on the floor, and Ellen was using the table. Betsy was painting a girl picking flowers, Ellen was painting a row of houses, and Billy, who always painted very fast, had just finished a landscape with cows. There were mountains in the background.

"Is that thing in the sky supposed to be the sun?" Ellen asked, looking down at Billy's painting.

"Sure, it's the sun," said Billy. "What does it look like?"

"Like a fried egg," said Ellen.

Betsy laughed, and came to look at Billy's painting. "It does look like a fried egg," she said.

"I don't care," said Billy. "I like it that way." He laid out a fresh piece of paper, and Betsy and Ellen returned to their painting.

Just then, the gas man came to read the gas meter. He knocked on the back door, and when Betsy's mother opened it the man went inside. In a moment he came out again. "Hot enough to fry an egg on the sidewalk today, all right," he called back to Betsy's mother, as he shut the screen door.

As the front gate closed, Ellen said, "Do you believe anybody really could fry an egg on the sidewalk?"

"Sure!" said Billy. "My father read in the paper last week that a man fried an egg on the sidewalk."

"I don't believe he fried it," said Betsy.

"I'll bet I could fry one," said Billy. "I'll bet I could

fry one right here on this step." Billy got up and put his hand on the wooden step of the summerhouse. "Feel it," he said. Both Betsy and Ellen felt the step. "Oh that isn't nearly hot enough," exclaimed Ellen.

"Well, feel the bricks in this path," said Billy. "Feel

the bricks, how hot they are." The girls felt the bricks. They were hotter than the step, but Betsy said, "Even they aren't hot enough."

"I'm going out front and feel the sidewalk," said Billy.

"What for?" asked Betsy. "You haven't any egg."

"And it wouldn't fry if you had," said Ellen. "The sidewalk isn't hot enough either."

"I'll get an egg and show you," said Billy. He ran to the kitchen door and called inside to Betsy's mother. "Do you have an egg I can have?"

Betsy's mother came to the door. "Whatever do you want with an egg, Billy?" she asked.

"I want to fry it on the sidewalk," said Billy.

"Billy," said Betsy's mother, "I am not going to give you one of my eggs for that."

Billy felt in his pocket and pulled out some pennies. "I could pay you for one," he said.

"No, my eggs are not for sale," replied Betsy's mother.

Billy counted his pennies. "Do you think I could buy one at the store for four cents?" he asked.

"I don't think so," said Betsy's mother. "Perhaps for five cents."

Billy went back to the summerhouse. "Anybody got a penny to put toward buying an egg?" he said.

"I don't have any," said Ellen.

"Neither have I," said Betsy.

"How about Star?" said Billy. "Did she spend the penny we gave her last week from the lemonade?"

"I don't know," said Betsy. "Star and Linda are playing with Lillybell over at Mrs. Jackson's."

Billy went to the back wall of the garden and climbed up on it. "Hey, Star!" he shouted. "Star!"

"What do you want?" Star called back from the porch of the Jacksons' house.

"Have you still got that penny?"

"Yes," replied Star.

"Do you want to help me buy an egg to fry on the sidewalk?" Billy shouted.

At this question, all three children—Star and Linda and Lillybell—rushed to the wall. "What did you say you're going to do?" asked Linda.

"I'm going to buy an egg and fry it on the sidewalk," said Billy. "That is, if you'll let me have your penny, Star."

"If I can fry the egg, I will," said Star.

"Sure, sure!" replied Billy.

Star reached into the deep pocket of her skirt, pulled out a tiny red purse, and opened it. It held just one penny. She took it out and handed it to Billy.

"Thanks!" said Billy, setting off for the nearest grocery store. Betsy and Ellen ran after him, followed by Star and Linda and Lillybell, who tagged along not far behind. They all gathered around Billy at the grocery counter.

"What can I do for all of you?" asked the man behind the counter.

"I want to buy an egg," said Billy.

"Just one?" asked the man.

"Yes, just one," replied Billy. "Because I only have five cents."

"Well, they're six cents apiece today," said the man.

Billy's face fell, and so did those of all his friends. "Oh!" said Billy. Then, after a moment, he said, "Don't you have one with a crack in it, or maybe one that's a little old?"

"No," replied the grocery man, "we don't have old eggs here—only strictly fresh eggs. But I'll look and see if there is one with a crack in it." He disappeared into a back room, but after a few minutes he returned. "Here's one," he said, "with just a little crack in it. If you carry it carefully, it will hold together." He put the egg in a small paper bag and handed it to Billy.

Billy gave the man the five pennies. "Thanks a lot," he said, as all six children left the store. They walked in a bunch toward Betsy's house, and soon they met a school friend, Kenny.

"Billy, where are you going with that gang of girls?" Kenny asked.

"I'm going to fry an egg on the sidewalk," replied Billy.

"You are?" exclaimed Kenny. "Well, I'm coming too." And Kenny joined the crowd.

At the next corner, they met Richard and Henry. "Hey," cried Kenny, "Billy's going to fry an egg on the sidewalk."

"This, I want to see," said Richard.

"Me, too," said Henry. They also joined the bunch of children.

"I'm going to fry it," said Star, but no one paid any attention to her. They were all talking at once.

"Where are you going to fry it?" asked Kenny.

"Over on our pavement," said Betsy.

As soon as they reached Betsy's, all the children began to feel the pavement for the hottest spot. Each one had a different idea about it, but at last they agreed that the hottest spot was right in the middle of the sidewalk in front of the gate. Star came running out of the house with the pancake turner in her hand.

"I'm all ready to fry it," she said, pushing her way into the center of the group.

Billy knelt down on the sidewalk and took the egg out of the bag. "Oh, I think we should clean the pavement first," Betsy cried, just as he was about to break it. "It will get full of dirt."

"O.K.," said Billy, and he dusted off the spot with his handerkerchief. Betsy and Linda and Star dropped down beside him, and Billy tapped the egg on the cement.

"There's an ant!" cried Ellen. "Don't put it on the ant."

Billy brushed the ant away. Once again he held the egg over the spot they had selected, but again a voice held him back. This time it was Lillybell. "You got to have bacon grease to fry an egg," she said. "How you going to fry it, without bacon grease? My mommy —she cooks for Mrs. Jackson—my mommy always fries eggs in bacon grease."

Billy sat back on his heels and thought about this.

Suddenly the eggshell broke in his hand, and the soft egg fell out onto the sidewalk.

"You haven't got any bacon grease," said Lillybell, shaking her head. "No bacon grease."

The children watched the egg, but nothing happened. It just lay there, its golden center floating in a little pool of egg white. Suddenly Billy called out. "Get up, everybody! Look at the shadow you're making. How can it fry if the sun doesn't shine on it?"

"Oh, there's a ladybug! There's a ladybug walking into it," Kenny shouted. He reached out and brushed the ladybug aside, just as the town-hall clock struck twelve. "That's time for my lunch," he added. "I have to go."

"So do we," said Henry. "I don't think that egg is going to fry anyway."

"Nope," said Lillybell. "Haven't any bacon grease."

Kenny and Richard and Henry left, and a few minutes later Betsy's mother came out. "Mother," said Star, "look at the egg. Billy is letting me fry it."

Mother looked down at the sidewalk. "What a mess!" she said. "You will have to clean it up, Billy, before you go home."

"I think it's beginning to fry," said Billy, kneeling again to look at the egg. "See, around the edge, Betsy."

Betsy, too, knelt down and examined the egg. "I don't see anything," she said. "Only some dust on it."

"You have to have bacon grease," said Lillybell.

"Come along now," said Betsy's mother. "I've made some sandwiches. You can all eat them in the summer-house."

"We'll have to take turns minding the egg," said Billy. "We can't go away and just leave it here. Somebody might step on it."

"Cover it over," said Ellen. "Get a box or a basket or something, and cover it over."

Billy went to the garage and came back with an old bushel basket. He turned it upside down and placed it over the egg. "Better put a sign on it," said Betsy. "Somebody might move it away."

Billy ran to the summerhouse and found a piece of white paper. With his paintbrush, he printed on it with red paint, *Do Not Move This. Egg Frying.* He tacked the sign on the basket with thumbtacks, and returned to the summerhouse.

Betsy was passing a large plate of peanut-butter-and-jelly sandwiches. Glasses of cold milk stood on a tray on the table. "Help yourselves to the milk," said Betsy. Each child took a glass and settled down to eat. Once, during lunch, Billy ran out front to make sure the basket was still there. He raised it up and looked under it. "It's O.K.," he said, running back to the summerhouse. "But, of course, the egg isn't frying now."

"Has to have bacon grease," mumbled Lillybell, her mouth full of sandwich.

The sandwiches disappeared, one by one. Betsy's mother brought another pitcher of milk and filled the empty glasses. Then she brought a plate of cookies. Betsy was nibbling one when she saw Thumpy coming up the drive.

"Where do you suppose he's been?" she said, as Thumpy came bounding toward the summerhouse, delighted to smell food. He went to Star for a piece of cooky.

"Go away, Thumpy," Star said. "Your ears are all wet."

"Thumpy," said Betsy, "have you been after the goldfish again?"

Thumpy was begging from Billy now. "Yeah, his ears are wet," said Billy, giving him a piece of cooky. "But it isn't water. It's something slippery, sort of sticky."

About five minutes later Mr. Kilpatrick, the policeman, stopped his red car in front of Betsy's house. He got out and picked up an old bushel basket that was lying on its side in the middle of the sidewalk. "And what's this?" he said, as he looked at the sign that was fastened to the basket—*Do Not Move This. Egg Frying.*

Mr. Kilpatrick pushed back his hat and scratched

ıis head. He looked all around on the sidewalk, but he lidn't see any egg. "Now what kind of an April Fool oke is this to be playing in the middle of July," he ;aid. "And blocking the pavement with an old basket, oo." He threw the basket into the back of his car. 'Only fit for the dump," he said, as he got in the car ınd drove off.

"Oh," cried Betsy, "I think Mr. Kilpatrick just drove ›y. I saw his red car."

Billy dusted cooky crumbs off his shirt. "Let's go ›ack and finish frying the egg," he said.

The children ran out front, Billy leading the crowd. Ie came to the place where the basket had stood. "It's ;one!" he cried. Then he looked at the pavement. "The gg's gone too!" he shouted. "They're both gone!"

All the children stared at the pavement. There was ıo egg. They looked all around. There was no basket. They stooped down and examined the sidewalk where hey had left the egg, but there was no sign that the egg ıad ever been there.

"I want my penny back," said Star. "You didn't let me fry the egg."

"Can't fry eggs without bacon grease," said Lillybell.

Suddenly Betsy remembered. "Thumpy!" she cried. "Thumpy, let me look at your ears!"

"Oh!" cried Billy. "He *ate* it! He ate it! That old Thumpy ate my egg!"

CHAPTER 5

A BELL FOR JIM DANDY

ONE afternoon Billy Porter was roller-skating on the sidewalk in front of his house when the Jim Dandy truck came up the street. The Jim Dandy truck sold Jim Dandies—ice cream on a stick. There were a great many different kinds of Jim Dandies. There was vanilla covered with chocolate, vanilla covered with nuts, vanilla covered with coconut. There was also chocolate ice cream covered with the same coatings. There were peach and strawberry Jim Dandies, and there were others made of orange ice and raspberry ice. These melted quickly, but they were pretty to look at. All the different kinds were kept frozen and as hard as bricks inside of the truck. When the driver took them out, they smoked as they struck the warm air. All the children liked to buy Jim Dandies.

The driver of the truck was always called Jim. This summer one of the high-school boys was driving the truck. His name was Doremus Freemantle, and he liked being called Jim for a change.

Billy watched the white truck as it drew nearer, wondering why he couldn't hear the bell ring. Usually he knew that the truck was in the neighborhood long before he saw it, because of the bell that rang every few seconds. He wished he had the money to buy a Jim Dandy, but he had spent his allowance for the whole week on a toy airplane that he had seen in a shop window a few days ago. The airplane was broken now, and Billy wished he had the money he had spent for it. I could have bought a Jim Dandy, thought Billy, if only I hadn't spent all my money.

The truck went very slowly. To Billy's surprise, he heard Jim shouting, "Jim Dandies! Jim Dandies!" But no one came running out of the houses, the way they usually did, to buy any. Billy skated toward the truck. "Hi!" he shouted. "Hello, Jim!"

"Hi, Billy," Jim called back.

"Why don't you ring your bell?" Billy called.

"It doesn't work," Jim answered. "I don't know what's the matter with it."

"Oh, that's bad," said Billy.

"Yep!" said Jim. "Haven't had many customers and I'm hoarse as an old bullfrog from shouting."

"Maybe I can help you," said Billy. "We have a bell. I'll see if I can find it." Billy started for home. Then an idea came to him. He turned around and skated back to the truck. "Jim," he called out, "if I can find the bell would you let me come along to ring it?"

"Sure!" replied Jim. "I'll even pay you."

Billy's face lit up like a lamp. "You will?" he said. "How much?"

"I'll give you a Jim Dandy," replied Jim. "Any flavor you want."

"Oh! That's great!" said Billy. "I'll take a chocolate one covered with chocolate." Then he said, "No, that chocolate's awful thin. I'll take a chocolate covered with nuts."

"Nothing doing yet," said Jim. "You get the bell first and do a little work. You're not going to get paid in advance."

"O.K.," said Billy. "I'll be right back." He skated off at top speed. At his front door he quickly unfastened his skates. "Mum!" he shouted. "Mum!"

"What do you want?" his mother called back.

Billy rushed upstairs to his mother. "Oh, Mum!" he said. "I've got a job! Where's our old bell?"

"What kind of a job do you have?" Mrs. Porter asked.

"I'm going to ring the bell for the Jim Dandy truck,"

said Billy. "Only I have to find a bell, 'cause Jim's bell is broken. Do you know where that bell is that was around here, Mum?"

"I haven't seen it for ages," said his mother.

"Well, will you help me find it, please?" Billy began looking on top of every table and chest and on every shelf. His mother pulled out drawers. They couldn't find the bell. Billy stopped hunting for a moment and looked out of the window. The truck was waiting right in front of the house. Billy ran into his own room. "I *have* to find it," he called to his mother. "I'll get a nice ride and I'm going to get paid, too. I'm going to get a chocolate Jim Dandy with nuts."

Just then Jim bellowed from out front, "Hey, Billy! Get a move on. I can't wait all day."

"I'm coming," Billy shouted back from the front window.

"Billy," said his mother, "I haven't seen that bell for ages. I think it may have been thrown away."

"Oh, Mum!" said Billy. "That's awful!" Then he

said, "Well, maybe I could take my flute. Do you think the flute would be all right?"

His mother looked very doubtful. "I don't think you can play a flute on an ice-cream truck," she said.

"Well, what about my drum?" he said.

"Hey, Billy!" came from out front. "I'm going on."

Billy picked up his flute in one hand and his drum in the other and dashed down the stairs. The screen door banged behind him as he ran out to the truck. "I couldn't find the bell," he called to Jim. "But I've got my flute and my drum."

"Flute!" cried Jim. "Who do you think I am, the Pied Piper?"

Billy hadn't thought of the Pied Piper, but now that Jim had mentioned him Billy remembered the old story. "Sure," said Billy. "All the children ran after the Pied Piper. You want the children to run after you, don't you?"

"Come along," said Jim, with a sigh. "Step lively. But don't forget it was the rats that came out first. I don't fancy a gang of rats running after the Jim Dandy truck." He reached down and took the drum out of Billy's hand. Then Billy climbed into the seat beside Jim.

"What shall I play?" asked Billy.

"What *can* you play?" said Jim.

"I can play 'Way Down upon the Swanee River,' " said Billy.

"That ought to make everybody jump," said Jim. "Anything else?"

"How about 'Little Drops of Water, Little Grains of Sand'?" asked Billy. "I just learned that."

"Won't do," Jim told him. "Everybody would think it was raining and go rushing for their umbrellas."

"Well, I can play 'Now the Day is Over,' " said Billy. "Only I don't play that so good."

"Skip it!" said Jim. "I have to sell a lot of Jim Dandies before this day is over."

"Oh," said Billy. "Well, how about 'Yankee Doodle'?"

"That's more like it," said Jim.

Billy put his flute to his lips and began to play "Yankee Doodle." He played it through twice. Then he said, "Anybody coming?"

"Not a soul," said Jim. Then he looked back. "Not even one rat."

"Shall I try the drum?" Billy asked.

"Well, it won't make things any worse," said Jim.

Billy laid his flute on the seat beside him and picked up his drum. He pulled the drumsticks out of the bands that held them fast to the drum and began to beat out a rhythm. After a minute or two he said, "See anybody coming?"

"What did you say?" Jim shouted back.

"I said do you see anybody coming?" Billy yelled, beating on the drum.

"No," shouted Jim.

"I'll do it harder," Billy screamed. He beat the drum until he was red in the face. "When do I get my chocolate Jim Dandy with the nuts?" he yelled.

"Not until we get a customer," Jim shouted at the top of his lungs.

Now the truck had turned into the street where Betsy lived. It rolled along slowly under the trees. Suddenly Billy had an idea. He stopped beating the drum and said, "Jim, stop right up there just beyond the fire-plug."

"Now what?" said Jim.

"Well, I have a friend who lives there," said Billy, "and I think maybe she has a bell."

Jim stopped in front of Betsy's house, and Billy jumped down. "Make it snappy," said Jim. "And don't come back with a violin."

"I'll be right back," said Billy.

Betsy and Star were playing in the summerhouse. They were surprised to see Billy. He ran up to them all out of breath. "Say, Betsy," he said, "have you got a bell?"

"A what?" said Betsy.

"A bell," said Billy. "You know, what you ring."

"Oh! A bell!" said Betsy. "What for?"

"Listen, Betsy, we're in an awful hurry," said Billy. "I'm helping Jim, and his bell is broken, and all I have is my flute and my drum, and they don't do any good."

Betsy looked puzzled. "What don't they do?" she asked.

"They don't bring the customers out, stupid," said Billy. "The customers don't come out and buy the Jim Dandies."

"Oh!" cried Betsy, "the Jim Dandies!"

"Sure," said Billy. "You see, I'm working for Jim and he's going to pay me, but not until I get a customer out. He's going to give me a chocolate Jim Dandy covered with nuts. They're much better covered with nuts, because the chocolate on the chocolate-covered ones is awful thin. So you get more if you get one covered with nuts."

Honk! Honk! went the horn at the front gate.

"Hurry up, Betsy," said Billy. "Hurry up and get me a bell.

"But I don't know where there is a bell," said Betsy. She started to run toward the back door of the house. Billy and Star followed. "I have my ukulele," said Betsy. "Don't you think maybe I could help with my ukulele?"

"You sure you haven't got a bell?" asked Billy.

Honk! Honk! went the horn.

"There's a bell on the alarm clock," said Betsy. "What about the alarm clock? It has a very loud bell."

"No, you'd have to keep winding it up all the time," said Billy.

"What about a sweet potato? I have a sweet potato," Betsy suggested. "That makes a pretty loud noise."

Honk! Honk! from Jim.

"Well, bring it along," said Billy, starting for the door.

"Wait for me!" cried Star from her room. "Wait for me!"

Billy and Betsy hurried down the driveway toward the truck. "Now remember," Billy whispered, "if he asks you to go along, the chocolate with nuts is the best."

"Well, did you get a bell?" Jim asked.

"Betsy's got a sweet potato," said Billy. "Blow it, Betsy. Let Jim hear it."

Betsy blew on the sweet potato. It screeched. "Very pretty," said Jim. "It sounds like the rats. Billy, you better stay here with your friend Betsy and make music."

Just then Star reached the truck. "Look!" she called out. Everyone looked. Star held up the triangle that she played in the kindergarten orchestra. She knocked it with her little rod. It sounded very much like the Jim Dandy bell before it was broken.

"Now that's something like it!" said Jim. "Baby, go ask your mama if you can come with me. That will get the customers out."

"She can't go without me," said Betsy.

"O.K.," said Jim. "Go ask your mother if you can both go."

Betsy ran back to the house. In a few minutes she came back with her mother. When Betsy's mother saw Jim she said, "Oh, it's you! Your mother told me you were driving the Jim Dandy truck this summer. Is there room enough for all of them?"

Jim grinned. "Yes," he said, "there's plenty of room."

"Will you get them back by five o'clock?" Betsy's mother asked.

"Yes, ma'am," Jim promised. "I'll take good care of them."

The three children climbed in beside Jim and they started off. Star insisted upon being the one to beat the triangle. Before they reached the corner a customer came out of one of the houses and bought five Jim Dandies. Billy's face fairly shone. "Some sale!" he said.

"Well, I guess you want your pay now," said Jim. "What kind did you say you wanted?"

Billy, Betsy, and Star all sang out together, "Chocolate with nuts." Jim handed them each a Jim Dandy. Then they had to take turns eating and beating the triangle.

Business was very good the rest of the afternoon. Promptly at five o'clock Jim set Betsy and Star down in front of their house. Then he opened the back of the truck and took out three more Jim Dandies. He handed one to each of the children. "Chocolate," he said, "with nuts."

CHAPTER 6

THE WATERMELON PARTY

One evening Betsy and her father were sitting in the summerhouse. Father was reading the paper, and Betsy was pasting stamps in her album. When it grew too dark to see clearly, Father laid his paper aside, and said, "Time to stop, Betsy."

"I've finished," said Betsy, getting up from the table. "Look, Father. Look at this beautiful stamp from

Japan. Billy Porter gave it to me. I gave him one that came from Egypt for it."

Betsy carried her stamp album to her father. He looked at the stamp and said, "That surely is a nice one." Betsy sat down on her father's lap. "My goodness, Betsy," he said, "you're getting too big to sit on my lap. Look where your legs come. Dangling way down, like macaroni."

Betsy laughed. "I'm never going to be too big to sit on your lap, Father," she said.

"Then I'm going to have to grow bigger," said Father.

Betsy leaned her head against her father's, and said, "Tell me about when you played in your grandfather's summerhouse."

"I think I've told you everything," Father replied.

"Think," insisted Betsy.

Father thought for a few minutes, and then he said, "Did I ever tell you about the watermelon parties we used to have?"

"Watermelon parties!" exclaimed Betsy. "You never told me! What's a watermelon party?"

"It's a party where you eat watermelon and plenty of it. You try to keep all of your seeds, because there's a prize that goes to the one who has the most seeds at the end of the party."

"Did you have the party outdoors?" asked Betsy.

"Oh, yes," replied Father, "and always in the evening. The summerhouse was the headquarters for the watermelons. That's where Grandfather cut them."

"I guess you have to have a watermelon party out of doors," said Betsy. "I guess it's pretty sloppy."

Father laughed. "Sloppy is a very good word for a watermelon party."

"How could you see to get the seeds out?" asked Betsy.

"We had Japanese lanterns strung all around on wires. It was a pretty sight."

"I wish I could have a watermelon party," said Betsy. "Do you think I could?"

"I don't see why not," replied Father. "But we ought to have Japanese lanterns. I can't imagine a watermelon party without Japanese lanterns."

"What happened to the ones your grandfather had?"

"I've no idea," said her father. "Perhaps they're packed away in your grandmother's attic. We could write and ask her."

"Oh, let's!" said Betsy. "Let's go in and write her now."

On Saturday morning Dolly and the parcel-post wagon stopped at Betsy's house. Mr. Fisher jumped down and lifted a big parcel out of the wagon. Betsy and Star came running from the summerhouse to see what was in the parcel. As soon as Mother looked at it, she said, "It's from Grandmother. It must be the Japanese lanterns."

"Oh, open it, Mother!" said Betsy. "Let's see!"

Mother cut the heavy cord on the parcel and pulled off the paper. Inside there was a brown carton. She lifted the flaps and took out some crumpled-up news-

paper. Star and Betsy knelt on the floor beside their mother and watched the unpacking. "Oh!" cried Star. "They're not lanterns. They're just flat hats."

Mother laughed. "They *are* lanterns," she said, shaking one out.

As it dropped open, the children saw that it really was a lantern. It was a beautiful one, made of oiled paper stretched over very thin bamboo hoops. It was decorated with pink and red flowers with green leaves. Star and Betsy watched as Mother removed each lantern. There were twenty-five of them and every one was beautiful. In the bottom of each one there was a place for a candle.

"Oh, Mother!" cried Betsy. "I can't wait to see them all lighted."

"Is it going to be Betsy's party or my party?" asked Star.

"It's going to be Betsy's party," replied Mother. "You don't have your parties in the evening. You have them in the afternoon."

"But I can come to Betsy's party, can't I?"

"If you can keep awake," said Mother.

"How many friends can I invite?" Betsy asked.

"Ask all of your friends who haven't gone away," said Mother.

"Shall I ask those new boys who just moved in next door to Billy Porter?" asked Betsy.

"Yes," replied her mother. "Mrs. Porter says they're nice boys."

"Jack is going to be in my room in school," said Betsy, "and I think little Rodney is awfully cute. Billy says Rodney's always up to something."

"Are the Wilson boys home?" asked Betsy's mother.

"Eddie is," said Betsy. "The twins went to camp, and Rudy is helping on his grandfather's farm. I'll invite Eddie."

Betsy lost no time spreading the news that she was having a watermelon party the following Saturday evening. As soon as Eddie Wilson heard of it, he came riding over on his bicycle to find out everything about the watermelon party. He found Betsy and Star in the summerhouse.

"Hi, Betsy," he said. "What are we going to do at your watermelon party?"

"We're going to eat watermelon," said Betsy.

"Sounds good," said Eddie.

"And everybody is going to count their seeds, and the one who has the most seeds, after we're through eating watermelon, will get a prize," said Betsy.

"How many pieces of watermelon do we get?" Eddie asked.

"As much as we want," said Betsy. "Father is going to get lots and lots of watermelons."

"Well, I can eat a lot of watermelon," said Eddie.

On his way home, Eddie passed this news on to his new friend Rodney. "I'll get the prize," said Eddie.

"How do you know you will?" asked Rodney.

" 'Cause I can eat more watermelon than anybody," said Eddie. "So I'll get the most seeds. It's simple."

When Eddie left, Rodney thought to himself, That

Eddie Wilson is awful cocky. Rodney thought about Eddie's boasting a long time. By afternoon he had decided upon a plan. He said to his mother, "Couldn't we have watermelon for dessert tonight?"

"If you want watermelon," his mother replied, "you go to the store on your bike and get one."

Rodney set off with the money that his mother had given him. When he reached the store he looked over the watermelons. "I'll take that one," he said to the storekeeper, pointing to the biggest one in the lot. Rodney handed his money to the man, and as the man gave him his change, Rodney said, "Do you think there are a lot of seeds in that watermelon?"

"I guess there are a good many," said the man.

Rodney couldn't lift the watermelon to put it in the basket on his bicycle. The storekeeper had to put it in for him. When he reached home, his mother had to help him carry it into the kitchen. Then she had to take almost everything out of the refrigerator in order to get the watermelon in.

When the watermelon was served at dinner, Jack and his father both said, "Oh, good! Watermelon!"

When dinner was over, Rodney said, "I'll help you clear the table, Mama." He carried the dessert plates out to the kitchen very carefully. "Mama," he said, "don't throw away the seeds. I want them."

"All of them?" asked his mother.

"Yes, all of them," replied Rodney.

"Whatever do you want with watermelon seeds?" his mother asked.

"I'm collecting them," said Rodney.

"You do collect the strangest things," said his mother, as she watched Rodney dropping the seeds into a jar.

As soon as all of the big watermelon had been eaten, Rodney persuaded his mother to let him go to the store for another one. By Thursday night everyone was fed up with watermelon except Rodney. "I don't want to see another piece of watermelon for a month," said his father.

"Betsy is having a watermelon party on Saturday night," said Rodney.

"I'm glad I'm not invited," said his father.

"What do we do at a watermelon party?" asked Jack.

"Eat watermelon, of course," said Rodney.

"What else do we do?" asked his brother.

"You'll find out," said Rodney.

Every evening Rodney carried the dishes from the dinner table, gathered up all the watermelon seeds, and put them in his jar. By Thursday he had a half-pint jar filled with black seeds. Rodney felt that whatever the prize at Betsy's party was going to be, it was already his.

On Saturday afternoon Rodney began to wonder how he could carry his watermelon seeds to the party without letting anyone see them. He decided to put them in a paper bag. He planned to stuff the bag of seeds into his pocket. He poured them from the jar into the paper bag and stood the bag on the window ill in his bedroom. The damp seeds began to make a wet spot on the bottom of the paper bag.

When it was time to leave with his brother Jack for he party, Rodney picked up the paper bag. To his

surprise, the bottom of the bag broke and the seeds fell to the floor in a shower. Rodney dropped on his hands and knees and began picking up the slippery seeds.

Rodney's father was going to drive the boys over to Betsy's house. Jack and his father were already in the car. "Hey, Rodney," Jack called, "get a move on. Billy's here. We're ready to go."

"I'm coming," Rodney called back, as he crawled around the floor.

In a minute he heard Jack shout again, "So long, Rodney, we're going."

"Half a minute and we're leaving," his father called out.

The faster Rodney tried to pick up the seeds, the more they slipped out of his fingers. He did not have anything to put them in, so he put them in his pocket. He was gathering up the ones that had rolled under the bed, when his father called out, "Time's up, Rodney. You can walk."

Before Rodney could get out from under the bed, he heard the car drive off. He scrambled to his feet and decided to leave the rest of the seeds where they were. Most of them were in his pocket. He dashed downstairs and ran up the street. He thought perhaps his father would be waiting for him around the corner. But when he turned the corner the car was out of sight. Rodney settled down to a fast trot. He held his hand over his pocket so that the seeds would not spill out.

It was a long way to Betsy's house, and now it seemed longer than ever. He could feel his legs moving, but he did not seem to be getting to Betsy's very fast. At last he reached Betsy's corner and turned into the street. Rodney could see a soft light shining out into the darkness of the street, but it was not until he reached the front gate that he saw what was making the light. Strung all over the yard, from tree to tree, were the beautiful Japanese lanterns. Rodney thought he had never seen anything more exciting than those Japanese lanterns. He ran the rest of the way. By the time he arrived, everyone was eating a piece of watermelon. "Hello, Rodney," Betsy called out when she saw him. "Come and get your watermelon from Father. He's over in the summerhouse."

Rodney went to the summerhouse. "Hello, young fellow!" said Betsy's father. "Here, take this piece." He handed Rodney a large paper plate with a big chunk of red, ripe watermelon on it.

Rodney looked at it. Then he said, "This piece doesn't have any black seeds. Can I have a piece with black seeds, please?"

"Sorry, son," said Betsy's father, "but these watermelons all have white seeds."

"No black seeds at all?" exclaimed Rodney.

"Not a one," said Betsy's father.

Rodney sat down with his piece of watermelon. He ate a few bites. He could hear Eddie Wilson say, "Oh, boy! Look at all these seeds. I'm ready for another piece."

"Never heard of watermelons with white seeds," Rodney muttered to himself. He took another bite. It was good watermelon, but somehow he had lost his appetite for watermelon. He watched the other children going to and from the summerhouse with their plates. He heard them shout to each other about the number of seeds that they were collecting. At last all the watermelons had been eaten, and the children laughed and squealed as they counted their slippery seeds.

"These white seeds are so little," said Ellen.

"Yes, they're harder to count than the big black ones," said Betsy.

Rodney just stood watching. He felt like an outsider, and he did not even bother to count the few white seeds that had come out of his piece of watermelon. He could feel the lump in his pocket made by the black seeds he had brought to the party. A whole pocketful, and they were no good! Rodney did not feel any better when he saw the prize that Eddie Wilson won—a beautiful little sailboat painted bright red. The inside was light blue. Ellen won the girls' prize. It was a doll with a suitcase full of clothes.

The children played games, but Rodney spent his evening kicking a stone up and down the garden path.

He never looked up at the Japanese lanterns. He didn't see the tiny lanterns of the fireflies twinkling in the bushes. He didn't smell the honeysuckle. He just kicked a stone.

Rodney was glad when the party was over and his father came to take him home. When he reached home he went right up to his room. As he walked through the door, he slipped on a watermelon seed. Down he went and bumped his nose. He began to cry. He sat on the floor and rubbed his nose, while the tears ran down his cheeks. In a few moments he got up, reached into his pocket, and pulled out a handful of watermelon seeds. He dropped them into the wastepaper basket, and said, "I hate watermelons!" Then he sobbed, and called out, "Mama!"

His mother came upstairs. "What's the matter, dear?" she asked.

"I fell down and bumped my nose," Rodney sobbed.

His mother put her arm around him, and said, "Let Mother look at it." Rodney lifted his face to his mother.

It was wet with tears, sticky from watermelon seeds, and very dirty. "There isn't anything the matter with your nose, dear," said his mother. "It's just dirty." Rodney cried harder than ever. "Oh, Rodney, didn't you have a good time at the party?" she asked.

"No!" sobbed Rodney. Then he told his mother the whole story about the watermelon seeds.

When he finished his mother held him tight, and said, "I'm glad you told me, Rodney. I don't believe you'll ever do anything like that again."

Rodney gulped. Then he said, "I'm sort of hungry."

"What would you like to eat?" asked his mother.

Rodney looked up at his mother, and said, "You don't happen to have a piece of watermelon in the refrigerator, do you?"

"I'll go see," said his mother.

CHAPTER 7

MUD IN THE EAR

IN THE middle of the summer, Betsy's neighbors, the Jacksons, decided to build a swimming pool. All the children in the neighborhood were interested, because they all hoped to be invited to swim in it when it was finished.

The wall at the back of the garden made a perfect grandstand from which to watch the building of the swimming pool. The day the steam shovel moved into the Jacksons' back yard, Betsy's summerhouse was empty. Betsy, Star, Ellen, Linda, Lillybell, Billy, Jack, and Rodney sat on the wall all morning, watching the workmen break up the surface of the ground with picks. The ground was very hard, because there had been no rain for two months and the hot sun had baked the earth, but soon the steam shovel was put to work. It lifted great bucketfuls of earth high into the air and emptied them into a truck. Dust blew all over the children, but they didn't notice it. In the afternoon they were back on the wall again.

"I can swim," said Rodney. "And so can Jack."

"So can I," said Billy.

"I can swim a little," said Betsy.

"Do you think Mr. Jackson will let us swim in his pool?" Billy asked Betsy.

"Maybe," Betsy said hopefully.

"Will I swim?" asked Star.

"Father will teach you," Betsy told her.

"Will he teach Ellen and me?" Linda asked.

"Maybe," said Betsy.

"When I see Mr. Jackson, I'm going to ask him if I can come over and swim," said Billy.

"So am I," said Rodney.

"Well, you'd better wait until he invites you," said Betsy.

"Yes," said Lillybell. "My mommy says, 'Mind your manners.' "

About four o'clock, Mr. Jackson appeared. As he went to speak to the men who were operating the steam shovel, he waved to the row of children sitting on the wall.

"I'm going to ask him now," said Billy.

"No, Billy," said Betsy, "you mustn't ask."

"Go ahead, Billy," said Rodney.

"Be quiet, Rodney," said his brother.

The children watched Mr. Jackson as he talked to the workmen. At last, he came over to them. "Mr. Jackson," said Rodney, "do you know what I would do if I had a big hole like that in my yard?"

"What would you do?" asked Mr. Jackson.

"I would make a swimming pool," said Rodney. "And I would let children swim in it."

"Are you making a swimming pool, Mr. Jackson?" Billy interrupted.

"Yes, I am," said Mr. Jackson.

"It will be deep, won't it?" asked Jack.

"I guess it will be too deep for children, won't it?" said Ellen.

"One end will be deeper than the other," said Mr. Jackson. "You can see how they are digging it out. See the little hill that runs from the shallow end to the deep end?"

The children all looked where Mr. Jackson was pointing. "Oh, yes," said Betsy.

"Who is going to swim in it?" Billy asked.

"Mrs. Jackson and I," said Mr. Jackson. "And, of course, we'll invite our friends to come."

"Do you have very many friends?" Rodney asked.

"Oh, yes, quite a lot," said Mr. Jackson.

"Do you have any children friends?" said Linda.

"Yes indeed," said Mr. Jackson.

"What are their names?" Star asked.

"Well, let me see," said Mr. Jackson. "Now there is one, sitting right there." He pointed to Lillybell, and Lillybell grinned. Mr. Jackson looked up at the sky and went on. "Then there's Betsy, and Star, and there's a young fellow named Billy Porter, and a curly-head named Ellen."

"And me?" piped up Linda.

"Yes, you," said Mr. Jackson, laughing. "And those two boys who moved next door to you, Billy."

"Us!" cried Rodney. "Jack and me?"

"That's right," said Mr. Jackson. "The very first day there is water in the pool, you can all come in."

"Thanks, Mr. Jackson," said Billy. "Thanks a lot!"

"Thanks, Mr. Jackson," the rest of the children chorused, as he went back to his house. Then the children ran home to tell their mothers about Mr. Jackson's pool.

"Mother," said Ellen, "Linda and I have to have

bathing suits, because Mr. Jackson has invited us to swim in his pool."

"That is very nice of Mr. Jackson," said her mother. "Linda can wear the suit you have outgrown, and I'll buy a new one for you."

When Billy Porter tried on the bathing trunks he had worn the summer before, he almost split the seams. The trunks were so tight he couldn't sit down. "I'll have to have some new ones," he told his mother. "I'm going to do a lot of swimming in Mr. Jackson's pool this summer."

At the end of the day, the men with the steam shovel went away, leaving a great pit in the ground. That night it began to rain. Betsy's father got up and closed all the windows. Betsy woke up. She could hear the thunder, and from her bed she could see the lightning flash. She could hear the trees blowing in the high wind and raindrops splashing on the windows. Then the rain came in great swirls that lashed the windows, and the noise it made drowned out the sound of the wind in the trees. After a while, the thunder and lightning passed. Betsy soon grew used to the sound of the downpour, and fell asleep.

It was still raining the following day, and it rained all day. It was the first day that summer that no one played in Betsy's summerhouse. It was too wet. Water poured off the furniture onto the wet, shining floor; it fell from the top step to the bottom in a waterfall, and crossed the soaked ground to the garden path, where it flowed down to the driveway in a stream and out into the street.

The next morning the sun was shining. After the rain everything seemed brighter than it had been before. The heavy dust on the leaves of the trees was washed away, and the grass, which had burned brown, showed patches of green. Everything was sparkling clean. As the sun rose higher, the morning grew hotter. Steam rose from the wet bricks in the path, as they turned from dark red to pink again. Late in the morning, Billy Porter rode over to Betsy's house on his bicycle. "Hey, Betsy," he said. "Let's go look at Mr. Jackson's swimming pool."

The two children ran to the wall and climbed up on it. To their great surprise, the big hole, dug only two days before, was full of water. "What do you know about that," cried Billy. "It's finished. We can go swimming."

"It looks awfully muddy," said Betsy.

"That will settle by this afternoon," said Billy. "Water always gets muddy when it rains."

"Not in swimming pools, it doesn't," said Betsy.

"What do you want?" said Billy. "It's a pool with water in it, isn't it?"

"It ought to be blue," said Betsy. "Swimming pools are always blue."

"Oh, don't be so fussy," said Billy.

When Billy reached home, he told Rodney and Jack the good news. "There's water in Mr. Jackson's pool. It's full. I'm going swimming this afternoon. Mr. Jackson said we could go swimming the first day there was water in the pool. Remember? You'd better come along." He went with them to ask their mother if they could go. "Is the pool finished so soon?" she asked.

"Billy says it's full of water," said Jack.

"You can go," said his mother. "But you can only go in the pool if Mr. or Mrs. Jackson is there."

"Oh, I think Mr. Jackson will be there," said Billy.

Right after lunch, the three boys rode over to the Jacksons'. They were wearing their bathing trunks. "I can't wait to get in that water," said Rodney.

"Me, too," said Jack. "Nice and clean and cool."

"Bet it looks nice," said Rodney. "I like the color of water in swimming pools. Is it blue, Billy?"

"Well, it didn't look very blue this morning," said Billy. "But maybe it will be bluer this afternoon."

The boys didn't stop at Betsy's; they headed straight for the Jacksons' house. They swung around the corner and there—to their great surprise—stood a fire engine, right in the driveway of the Jacksons' house. Its pumps were working. As they chug-chugged, muddy water gushed into the gutter. The boys jumped off their bicycles and ran to the fire engine. "Is the house on fire?" Billy shouted to one of the firemen.

"No," replied the fireman. "We're just pumping water out."

"Out of where?" asked Billy.

"Out of that hole they dug for a swimming pool," said the fireman.

"But we're going swimming," said Rodney.

"Not today, you're not," said the fireman. "You'll have to wait until the pool is built. The heavy rains started an underground spring flowing, and the hole filled up with water."

"Well, isn't that good?" said Billy.

"No, it isn't," said the fireman.

"You mean there isn't going to be any swimming pool?" said Jack.

"I guess there'll be a pool," said the fireman, "but it has to be built right. Can't have just a hole in the ground with a lot of muddy water."

Rodney went over to the fireman. "Would you let me sit on the fire engine?" he asked.

"Sure, if you want to," said the fireman.

Rodney climbed up into the driver's seat, and Billy and Jack followed. "This is even better than swimming," Billy said, when they were settled in a row on the long seat.

"Yes," said Jack. Rodney didn't say anything, but his face was beaming.

After all the water was pumped out, the boys climbed down from the engine and watched it drive away. Then they went to look at the big pit that had just been emptied. The uneven bottom and the sides of the hole were slimy with yellow-brown mud.

"Look!" cried Billy, as they peered down into it. "You can see the water bubbling up on the bottom. I guess that's the spring."

Rodney began running along the edge of the pit. "Where is it?" he cried. "I don't see it."

Billy pointed. "Right there," he said.

By this time, Rodney was down at the shallow end of the hole. "I don't see it," he said. Then suddenly his foot slipped in the mud. He slid right down the side of the pit into the slimy bottom, rolling over and over as he tumbled down the little hill that ran from the shallow end of the pit to the deep end. Rodney screamed, and Jack screamed too. "Get up, Rodney! Get up!" he cried.

Rodney struggled to his feet. He was dripping with mud. He tried to walk from the deeper part of the pit to the shallow part, but the bottom was so slippery that he couldn't get a foothold in the soft mud. "Come help me!" he yelled.

Jack ran to the shallow end of the hole and let himself down over the edge. He reached for his brother's hand, but they both slipped. Down Jack went, into the mud with Rodney. When they finally got to their feet, they looked like two gingerbread boys. Together, they slipped and slid their way to the shallow end of the pool. Billy stood on the bank, shouting directions to them. "Hoist him up, Jack," he shouted, "and I'll pull him out."

Billy kneeled down in the mud at the side of the pit. He reached down and took Rodney's hand. He pulled while Jack pushed, and Rodney came up over the edge so suddenly that Billy landed flat on his back. He got up and helped Jack out. Now Billy was almost as muddy as Jack and Rodney.

Just then Mr. Jackson appeared. When he saw the three boys he began to laugh. "What a sight you are!"

"Rodney slipped," said Billy.

"Looks to me as though Rodney was not the only one who slipped," said Mr. Jackson. "Come along, and I'll see if I can clean you up. I guess the hose would be best." The boys followed Mr. Jackson to the flower garden. "Now, stand still until I wash the mud off," he said, picking up the garden hose. But they didn't stand still. As soon as the spray touched them, they began jumping all around. The water was terribly cold and it tickled, but in a few minutes they began to enjoy the

shower bath. When they were finally clean and most of the water had dripped off their trunks, they got on their bicycles and rode home.

"Well, did you have a good time?" Rodney and Jack's mother asked them.

"Oh, yes," said Rodney, "it was great!"

"Get out of those trunks and put on your clothes," said his mother. "Daddy will be coming home any minute."

At dinner, their father said, "I hear that you two were in the pool today. How was it?"

"Well, Daddy," said Jack, "you see, there's a spring in it."

"There is?" said his father.

"Yes," said Jack, "and the pool was full of water."

"Most pools are," said his father.

"But this wasn't the right kind of water," said Jack.

"It wasn't blue water," piped up Rodney.

"Oh?" said his father.

"No, it wasn't blue at all," said Jack.

"And we sat on the fire engine, Daddy," said Rodney. "The firemen let us sit on it a long time, didn't they, Jack?"

"Yes, they let us sit on it until all the water was out," said Rodney.

"Out of where?" said his father.

"Just like I'm telling you, Daddy," said Jack. "Out of the pool."

"I saw the spring, Daddy," said Rodney. "I saw it bubble up."

"It was fun under the hose, wasn't it, Rodney?" said Jack.

"Yes," said Rodney. "That was fun."

"Well," said their father, "I'm glad you had such a good time. But what you did is just as clear as mud to me."

Later, when it was time for the boys to go to bed, Rodney went to say good night to his mother. She leaned over and looked at him. "Rodney," she cried, "you have mud in your ear!" Then she looked carefully at Jack. "And you, too," she said. "There's mud in your hair. To the bathtub with both of you!"

"It was sort of muddy over at Mr. Jackson's," said Jack.

"Yeah, sort of," said Rodney, digging the mud out of his ear.

CHAPTER 8

BETSY AND ELLEN GO TO MARKET

About half a mile from Betsy's house there was a big supermarket. Betsy loved to go with her mother when she shopped in the supermarket. There were so many nice things to do. Mother let her push the wire cart and help herself to the things on the shelves. When she leaned over the frozen-food chests, she felt the icy air that rose up and chilled her face.

It was fun to pick out the reddest apples, the biggest oranges, and the ripest pears. She liked to look over the shelves where the cereal boxes were piled up, to see if there was a new kind that she had not tried yet. She liked the slot machine filled with salted peanuts that emptied out a handful for a penny. It was exciting to drop a nickel into the big soda-pop machine and have the bottle drop into her hand. But the thing she liked best was meeting her friends. She hardly ever went into the supermarket without meeting at least one friend. Sometimes there would be a crowd of six or seven, all from Betsy's school, gathered around the soda-pop machine.

Usually Betsy's mother drove to market in the car. Then she piled the big bags, filled with all kinds of food, on the back seat. But when Father had the car, Mother walked to market. Then she took a wire cart on little wheels. It folded up when it was empty. She could either push it or pull it. Sometimes she sent Betsy with the cart and a list of the things she was to buy.

One morning Betsy's mother decided to make some vegetable soup. Father had taken the car, so she said to Betsy, "Betsy, I need some things from the supermarket. I want to make some vegetable soup."

"Oh, good!" said Betsy.

"Take the cart," said Mother. "I have the list all ready. Don't lose it."

Betsy started off. She pulled the cart behind her. Just as she reached the door of the supermarket, she met Ellen and Linda. Ellen was pulling a small express wagon. "Hello, Ellen," Betsy called out, when she saw her friend.

"Hello, Betsy," said Ellen, "are you going into the supermarket?"

"Yes," said Betsy. "My mother is going to make vegetable soup."

"My mother is going to make gingerbread," said Ellen.

"I have five cents for a bottle of soda and a penny for peanuts," said Linda.

The three children pushed through the swinging doors. Betsy held the door open so that Ellen could bring the wagon inside. "Now, Linda," said Ellen, "you sit in the wagon, right here by the door, and wait until I get all of the things."

"But I want to go with you and see everything," said Linda.

"Now, Linda!" said Ellen. "You know that Mama said you could have the soda and the penny for peanuts if you would mind the wagon."

"Can I have the soda now?" asked Linda.

"All right," said Ellen.

"I'm going to have one too," said Betsy.

The three children went over to the soda machine. Betsy had taken her mother's list out of her pocket. She laid it down on the window sill beside the soda machine, in order to get a nickel out of her purse. Then she poked the coin into the slot and took the bottle that appeared.

Ellen laid her list on top of a pile of canned soup.

The first bottle that she got, she gave to Linda. The second one she began drinking herself. The three children drank their sodas slowly. Linda sat in the wagon and Betsy and Ellen leaned against the machine.

When they finished, Linda said, "I'll sit right here in the wagon, Ellen. Right here beside the peanuts. Then when I want to put my penny in, I can put it in."

"All right," said Ellen. "I won't be long." Ellen looked around for the paper that she had laid down somewhere. She saw a slip on the window sill and picked it up.

Betsy placed her empty soda bottle in a container that was nearby. Then she looked around for the list that Mother had given her. She did not remember where she had put it. She looked on the window sill, but it wasn't there. She looked on the floor, but it wasn't there, either. Then she saw a piece of paper lying on top of a pile of cans. She picked it up, feeling happy that she had not lost Mother's list.

Ellen pushed one of the store's carts in front of

her. She looked at the list in her hand. *One dozen oranges,* she read. She pushed the cart to a big counter piled high with oranges and put twelve into the cart. She never thought of the crate of oranges that had arrived at her house only yesterday from her uncle in Florida.

Betsy looked at the list in her hand. She read, *A box of bird seed.* Betsy wondered what her mother wanted with bird seed. They did not have any bird. But she looked over the shelves until she found bird seed. The package had a picture of a canary on it.

Soon Ellen had collected three large onions, a bunch of celery, a bunch of pot herbs, a bunch of parsley, a bunch of carrots, half a pound of string beans, half a pound of lima beans, a can of tomatoes, three turnips, a beef bone, and two pounds of soup meat. The next thing on the list was two cans of dog food. Ellen pushed her cart around until she found the counter with the dog food. She took two cans. She probably would have remembered that they did not own a dog, but at that moment Linda let out a piercing scream. "Ellen! Ellen!" she yelled.

Ellen turned and looked toward Linda. She was standing in front of the peanut machine. She was holding her little hands like a cup under the opening. Her hands were full and peanuts were falling in a shower. They were rattling down and the great big jar that had held the peanuts was almost empty. Ellen left her cart and rushed to Linda. Just as Ellen reached her, the shower of peanuts stopped, for the jar was empty. "Look, Ellen!" said Linda. "Look what I got for a penny!" Ellen looked. The whole big jar of peanuts had emptied itself into the express wagon, although many had bounced onto the floor.

Linda's screams had caused a lot of excitement in the supermarket. The manager came running. Ellen looked up at him, and said, "I'm sorry, but my little sister didn't mean to break the peanut machine."

"She didn't break it," said the man. "It must be out of order. Don't worry about it. It wasn't her fault."

"What shall we do with all these peanuts?" asked Ellen.

"I can't put them back," said the man. "You might as well take them with you."

Every child in the store gathered around Linda and the express wagon. Some of the boys began to help themselves to the peanuts. "Leave my peanuts alone," said Linda. Then, to everyone's surprise, Linda sat down in the wagon and covered up the peanuts with the full skirt of her dress. "Hurry up, Ellen," she said. "Let's go home."

Ellen went back to her cart. She looked at her list again. The last thing was the dog food, so she hurried to the checking-out counter to pay for all the things she had bought. Her thoughts were full of peanuts. Ellen went through quickly, and she called out to Betsy, who was behind her, "Make Linda get off those peanuts and take a handful for yourself."

Betsy ran over to Linda. She stuck her hand under Linda's skirt and picked up a handful of peanuts.

"Thanks!" she said, and went back to the place where she had left her cart.

"Good-by," said Ellen.

" 'By," said Betsy. Betsy had now reached the end of her list. Beside the bird seed, she had a can of molasses, a package of brown sugar, a bag of flour, a box of ginger, a box of cinnamon, and a dozen eggs. In a few minutes she was on her way home. She pushed the cart ahead of her and nibbled on her handful of peanuts.

As she went in the back door of the house, she said, "Oh, Mother! You should have seen what happened to Linda. She put a penny into the slot for peanuts, and all of the peanuts came out and fell right into Ellen's express wagon. The whole big jarful, Mother!" As Betsy talked about the peanuts, she took the things that she had bought out of the cart and placed them, one by one, on the kitchen table.

Her mother's eyes grew larger and larger as she watched Betsy, until at last she saw the box of bird

seed with the picture of the canary on it. "Betsy," she said, "what on earth have you bought?"

"Everything that was on the list," said Betsy.

Her mother looked over the things on the table. "But none of these things were on the list," she said. "What would I want with bird seed for canaries? We haven't a canary. And where is the dog food for Thumpy and all the things for the vegetable soup?"

Betsy looked puzzled. She felt in her pocket and pulled out the list. "Here's the list, Mother," she said.

Her mother took the piece of paper. She looked at it and said, "But this isn't the list I gave you. It isn't even my handwriting."

Just then the telephone rang. Betsy ran to answer it. It was Ellen. "Betsy," asked Ellen, "did you get the wrong things for your mother?"

"Yes," said Betsy.

"I did too," said Ellen. "My mother says she sent me for things to make gingerbread, and I just brought home a lot of vegetables and some dog food."

"Well, my mother doesn't like what I brought home one bit," said Betsy.

"I think it will be all right," said Ellen. "My mother says if your mother will make the gingerbread, my mother will make the vegetable soup, and then you can all come over here for supper and bring the gingerbread."

"Oh, that's wonderful!" said Betsy. "Wait, I'll call Mother."

Betsy's mother came to the telephone, and Ellen's mother got on the other end. She repeated what Ellen had said to Betsy. "Well, I guess that *is* much easier than exchanging all the things," said Betsy's mother.

"Linda will be disappointed," said Linda's mother. "She wants to go right back and put a penny in the gumdrop machine."

HI DIVE SHWIMING CLUB

CHAPTER 9

THE SWIMMING CLUB

IT TOOK a long time to build the swimming pool. The mud dried up, and the spring disappeared. Only a stake driven into the bottom of the big pit showed the place where the water had bubbled up. Men came and looked at it and went away. The hot sun baked the earth so that big cracks appeared all over the bottom of the hole. Mr. Jackson would not allow the children to go into his place at all, for fear they might fall in the pit. He had not forgotten the gingerbread boys.

At last a crew of workmen came and laid the bottom of the pool. They made it so strong that no spring could ever burst through. As soon as the cement mixer arrived, the children sat in a row up on the wall. They loved to watch the cement mixer grind round and round like a giant animal chewing its cud. Finally the painters came to paint the bottom and sides of the pool. The children were all on the wall again. They watched as the cement changed from gray to a deep sky-blue. Meanwhile, carpenters were busy building two bathhouses beside the garage.

Then the day came when the pool was filled with water for the first time. Betsy and her friends sat on the garden wall watching the water creep nearer and nearer to the top of the pool. Mr. Jackson stood leaning against the wall near the children.

"It's the prettiest blue water I ever saw," said Betsy.

"I can't wait to get in it," said Billy.

"Me too!" said Rodney.

"Do you know what?" said Billy. "I've got an idea."

"What is it?" Betsy asked.

"Well, I think we ought to have a club—a swimming club."

"Yes," shouted Rodney, "let's have a swimming club."

"And Betsy's summerhouse can be our clubhouse," Billy went on.

"Won't we do anything but swim?" Ellen asked.

"Oh, sure! We'll do lots of things," said Billy. "But we won't let anybody swim in our pool who isn't a member. Anybody who isn't a member has to pay to swim in our pool."

The children were all delighted with this idea. They liked anything that had to do with collecting money. "How much do you think we ought to charge?" Betsy asked.

"Twenty-five cents," said Billy.

"I think that's too much," said Ellen. "I think fifteen cents is enough."

Billy jumped down off the wall and faced the others. "We'll have to vote on it," he said. "Now, all in favor of charging twenty-five cents hold up your hand." Rodney, Star, and Lillybell all held up their hands.

The only reason Linda didn't put hers up was because Ellen hadn't held up her hand.

"Now, all in favor of charging fifteen cents hold up your hand," said Billy. Jack, Betsy, Ellen, and Linda held up their hands. Star and Lillybell put theirs up again. "Star and Lillybell are too little to be in the club," said Billy. "They don't even know how to vote."

"Yes," said Rodney, "clubs have to have secrets, and they're too little to keep secrets. Star and Lillybell can't be in this club."

Star and Lillybell both began to cry. Star got down off the wall on one side, and Lillybell got down on the other. Star ran home, crying, "I want to be in the club. I want to be in the club." Lillybell ran to the kitchen door of the Jacksons' house, crying, "Mommy! They won't let me be in the club!"

Billy looked at Linda and said, "I think she's too little to be in the club, too." Linda opened her mouth and shrieked. In a moment her whole face was running with tears.

"She has to be a member," said Ellen. "If Linda can't be a member, I won't be a member."

"And if Ellen isn't a member, I won't be a member," said Betsy. "And then you can't use my summerhouse for a clubhouse."

"Oh, O.K.," said Billy. "But if Linda tells any club secrets, she'll be put out of the club."

"I won't tell," said Linda.

"What shall we name the club?" asked Rodney.

"We could call it the Blue Water Swimming Club," said Betsy.

"No," said Billy, "that isn't good enough."

"How about High Dive Swimming Club?" Jack suggested.

"Oh, that's good," Billy exclaimed. "High Dive Swimming Club."

"But I don't know how to dive at all," said Betsy.

"I don't even know how to swim yet," said Ellen.

"High Dive Swimming Club," Billy repeated. "H.D.S.C. They're our letters. H.D.S.C."

"What does it mean?" asked Linda.

"High Dive Swimming Club," said Billy. "And that's the most important secret."

"Oh!" said Linda.

"That will be our password," said Billy. "The password to get into the clubhouse or into the pool is H.D.S.C."

"Now, Linda," said Rodney, "don't you go tell that secret." Linda looked at Rodney with big eyes, but she didn't say a word.

Everyone was pleased to be a member of the swimming club, and they had forgotten all about Star and Lillybell. "Now let's make a sign and put it on our clubhouse," said Billy. "We have to have the name of the club on the clubhouse." The children jumped down from the wall and ran to the summerhouse.

Mr. Jackson, who had been leaning against the wall all this time, walked away and went into his house.

"I'll get some paper and my paints," said Betsy, running off to find them. Soon she was back with a piece of cardboard and a bottle of blue paint. She spread the cardboard on the table and took the top off the bottle of paint.

"Make it big, Betsy," said Billy.

"I will." Betsy made a big blue *H*. Then she made an *I*. This she followed with a large *D*.

"Say," said Billy, "that's not the right way to spell 'high.'"

"Well, that's the way I like to spell it," said Betsy, making another *I*. Billy watched her make a *V*. Then he said, "Don't forget the *E*. That's one of those words with an *E* on it."

"I know," said Betsy. "You don't have to tell me how to spell." Betsy made the *E*. Then she left a little space and put down an *S*, but she started it wrong and made it backwards. "What's that?" asked Billy.

"An *S*," said Betsy. "You spell swimming with an *S*. I suppose you think you spell it with a *C*."

"It's a funny-looking *S*," said Billy.

Betsy bent her head over her work. After the funny-looking *S,* Betsy made an *H.* "Hey!" cried Billy. "What are you doing?" Betsy looked up. "I wish you'd leave me alone, Billy. Let me do this sign."

"She's spelling it wrong," said Billy to the rest of the children.

"I am not," said Betsy. "It's s-h-w-i-m-i-n-g—swimming."

There was a big argument over this. Jack said Betsy was right, Ellen wasn't sure, Rodney didn't know, and Linda was not asked. When the sign was finished it said *Hi Dive Shwiming Club.*

"Now we have to put it up," said Betsy.

Billy, as usual, found thumbtacks in his pocket. Betsy and Jack brought the ladder from the garage, and while Ellen and Betsy held the ladder, Billy pinned the sign over the entrance to the summerhouse. Linda looked up at the sign. "What does it say?" she asked her sister.

"High Dive Swimming Club," said Ellen.

Linda sucked her finger and looked at the sign. Then

she took her finger out of her mouth and said, "I thought the name was a secret." This threw the rest of the club members into a dither.

"Sure! She's right!" cried Jack. "It's supposed to be a secret. You know—H.D.S.C."

Up went the ladder again. Up went Billy. Down came the sign that said *Hi Dive Shwiming Club*. Now it was five o'clock and Betsy's mother put the whole crowd into the back of the car and drove them to their homes.

The following afternoon was the time they had looked forward to ever since Mr. Jackson had begun to build the pool. This was the day they were to get into that beautiful blue swimming pool. Billy was the first to arrive at Betsy's house. He had his swimming trunks with him. When Betsy saw him she called out, "Hello, Billy. Password, please. Password!"

"H.D.S.C.," Billy called out. Then he held up his swimming trunks and said, "Look!" Betsy looked at his blue trunks. Down the right leg were the four letters

H.D.S.C. They were bright red. "Oh, Billy," cried Betsy, "you've got the letters on."

"Yes," said Billy. "I couldn't sew 'em on, so I just used some Scotch tape. I think they'll stay."

Then Rodney and Jack arrived. "Password!" cried Billy and Betsy together.

"H.D.S.C.," said Jack.

"H.D.S.C.," said Rodney. When the two brothers saw the letters on Billy's trunks, they both wished that they had thought of doing the same thing.

"I hope somebody comes who isn't a member of our club," said Jack. "Then we'll get fifteen cents."

"Star and Lillybell aren't members," said Rodney.

"Well, I don't think we can make Star and Lillybell pay fifteen cents," said Betsy, "because Star is my sister and Lillybell lives at the Jacksons', and anyway they were invited."

"What do you mean, they were invited?" asked Rodney.

"Mr. Jackson invited them," said Betsy.

"I don't think that makes any difference," said Billy. "They're not in the club. I think we ought to vote on it."

At that moment Ellen and Linda arrived. "Password! Password!" the others called out to them.

"H.D.S.C.," said Ellen.

"Linda," said Billy, "give the password."

"D.D.D.D.," said Linda.

"She doesn't even know the password," cried Billy. "She shouldn't be a member of the club. She can't remember the password."

"Where's Star?" said Linda.

"She went to play with Lillybell," said Betsy.

The club members now made their way to the back wall. The big moment had come. They were going into the pool at last. They all scrambled over the wall. Then they turned to the pool. There, fastened to a rake that had been stuck in the ground, was a sign. It said *Jacksons' Pool. H.D.S.C. Members Keep Out.*

The children were struck dumb. They stood in a

quiet bunch, looking at the pool. Star and Lillybell and Mr. Jackson were in it. Lillybell was floating around in a rubber tire, and Mr. Jackson was holding Star by the back of her bathing suit. "Now kick your legs. That's right. Kick hard," he was saying.

Linda wondered why the club members were so quiet. She put her hand in Ellen's and said, "What's the matter, Ellen?"

"Sh!" said Ellen.

The club members walked around the pool almost on tiptoe. At the shallow end they stood in a line, looking down at the three in the pool. Finally Mr. Jackson looked up. "Hi there!" he said.

"Hello!" said the children, in very weak voices. There were tears in Betsy's eyes, and Ellen was biting her lower lip. Billy's face was red, and Rodney was already rubbing his eyes with his fists. Jack's face was very long.

"Billy," said Mr. Jackson, "whose swimming pool is this?"

"Yours, Mr. Jackson," replied Billy.

"Betsy," said Mr. Jackson, "who does this swimming pool belong to?"

"You, Mr. Jackson," said Betsy.

"Rodney," said Mr. Jackson, "who owns this swimming pool?"

"You do, Mr. Jackson," Rodney answered.

"What do you think, Jack?" said Mr. Jackson.

"Oh, it's yours, sir," said Jack.

"And what is your opinion, Ellen?" said Mr. Jackson.

"It's yours, Mr. Jackson," replied Ellen.

Before Mr. Jackson could say anything to Linda, she piped up, "I knowed it was your swimming pool, Mr. Jackson. I knowed it all the time."

"Good!" said Mr. Jackson. "See that none of you forget it! Now go put your bathing suits on."

The children dashed to the bathhouses. They were out again in a flash. As Billy came out of the bathhouse, he pulled the letters *H.D.S.C.* off his trunks and tossed them behind a bush. When he reached the pool, he jumped in with a big splash. As he struck out into the water, he said, "Mr. Jackson, you don't spell it s-h-w-i-m-i-n-g, do you?"

"No, you don't," said Mr. Jackson. "But if you did, I would say that you are a very good shwimer."

CHAPTER 10

BETTY JANE'S SALT-WATER TAFFY

SCHOOL opened the second week in September. Now Betsy's friends could gather in the summerhouse only on Saturdays. Soon the yellow leaves began to fall. They fell into Mr. Jackson's swimming pool and had to be skimmed off with a rake. Some sank to the bottom and turned brown. The air felt cool when the children came out of the water. They didn't go in very often.

One evening Betsy's father said, "Betsy, how would you and your crowd like to go on a hay ride?"

"A hay ride," exclaimed Betsy. "Oh, Father, that would be wonderful! I've never been on a hay ride."

"I think it's about time you went on one," said her father. "A man in my office lives on a farm, and he says that his farmer can let us have one of the hay wagons."

"When can we go?" Betsy asked.

"I thought next Saturday afternoon would be a good time to go," said her father. "We can take a picnic supper and get back early in the evening."

"How many friends can I ask?" said Betsy. "Is it a big wagon?"

"I guess ten would be about right," her father replied. "With you and Star, that would make twelve children and we'll have to have a few grownups along too."

"Let's ask Mr. and Mrs. Jackson," said Betsy, "'cause they've been so nice letting us use the swimming pool."

"Yes, we'll invite them to go with us," said her father.

Betsy began counting on her fingers the ten friends she would ask. "There's Ellen and Linda and Billy," she said, "and Rodney and Jack." She moved to her other hand. "And Mary Lou and Betty Jane, if her mother will let her. Betty Jane has to be careful."

"Careful of what?" said her father.

"She's delicate," said Betsy, going back to counting on her fingers. "Then there's Kenny and Christopher. She has to wear her rubbers."

"Who has to wear rubbers?" said her father.

"Betty Jane," replied Betsy.

Betsy held out her remaining little finger. "Oh, Father," she said, "I only have one finger left for all the Wilson boys. There are four. I can't ask Eddie Wilson without inviting his twin brothers, because they're in my room in school, and I can't ask the twins and leave Rudy out, even though he is older."

"Well," said Father, "throw in all the Wilson boys. We can sit tight."

"Oh, Father," Betsy exclaimed, "we forgot Lillybell!"

"Can't forget Lillybell," said her father. "We'll have to sit tighter."

Betsy's friends were delighted when they heard about the hay ride. When Betsy asked Betty Jane if she could go, Betty Jane said, "I'll have to ask my mother. She's very particular about what I do, because I have to be careful."

The next day Betty Jane rushed up to Betsy as soon as she reached school. "I can go on the hay ride, Betsy," she announced, "if it's a nice day."

"Well, of course," said Betsy, "we won't go if it rains."

The day before the hay ride it did rain, and Betty Jane was not the only one who was worried about the hay ride. All the children who had been invited wondered whether the hay ride would come off. But when the morning dawned, the sun was shining and the air was fresh and cool. By afternoon it was much warmer, but the children brought sweaters with them. They all met at Betsy's house.

Betty Jane arrived with a box under her arm. Everyone noticed the box, for across the lid in big letters it said *Salt-Water Taffy*. There were pictures of salt-water taffy all over the lid too, so that there was no mistaking what was inside. There was beautiful pink and pale-yellow and chocolate-colored salt-water taffy. There was white salt-water taffy with red stripes. All the children had had salt-water taffy at some time or other, and they all knew that it was very good.

When Betty Jane climbed into Mr. Jackson's car, everyone else tried to get into Mr. Jackson's car with her, until Betsy said, "Everybody can't ride in that car. Somebody has to ride in our car."

Then there was a great deal of shouting. "You go in the other car." No, I was here first." "You were not." "Move over. Move over." "There's no room for me."

"Get out of there. I was sitting beside Betty Jane." This came from Eddie Wilson.

"Well, if you'll just move over, I can sit on the other side of Betty Jane." This came from Mary Lou.

Finally everyone was settled. There were eleven in Mr. Jackson's station wagon. The rest were in the other car with Betsy and Star and their father and mother. Star and Linda were in the front seat, with Star on her mother's lap. Betsy, Rodney, Ellen, Jack, and Billy sat in the back.

They hadn't gone far when Linda said, "Did you see the big box of salt-water taffy that Betty Jane brought?"

"How do you know it's salt-water taffy?" asked Betsy's father. "You can't read."

"I saw the pictures," said Linda.

In the trunk of the car there were cartons filled with the picnic supper and a big thermos bottle of hot cocoa. There were hot dogs to roast over a fire and there were big soft rolls. There were baked beans and a big pot to heat them in. There were pickles and apples and plums. There were gingerbread and spongecake. The hay wagon would take them to a real picnic place with outdoor fireplaces for cooking.

When they reached the farm where the hay wagon was waiting for them, the children jumped out of the cars and ran up to it. The farmer was just leading two strong horses out of the barn. Everyone stood by and watched him as he hitched the horses to the wagon.

Billy turned to Mary Lou and said, "I've never been in a hay wagon."

"Neither have I," said Mary Lou. "I've never been in any kind of a wagon."

"Oh, I have," said Betsy. "I've been in a wagon on my grandfather's farm."

Finally the horses were hitched to the wagon, and the children could climb in. As Betty Jane was about to climb up, Billy said, "Here, Betty Jane. You better let me hold that box for you." Betty Jane handed the box to Billy. He looked at it while Betty Jane was helped up by Rudy. Billy could feel his mouth watering.

When Betty Jane was safely in the wagon, she reached down for her box and Billy handed it up to her. As soon as she was settled in the hay, there was a rush to sit beside her. Mary Lou flopped down on one side and Rodney got on the other side. Betty Jane placed the box between her legs as she stretched them out into the bed of hay on the bottom of the wagon.

The children kept looking at the box. Rodney's eyes seemed glued to it. "That's a pretty box," he said at last. "That salt-water taffy looks real."

"Yes," said Betty Jane. "My Aunt Mabel sent it to me from Atlantic City."

"It's a big box, isn't it?" said Mary Lou.

"Yes," said Betty Jane.

"Don't lose it in the hay," said Eddie.

"Oh, no," chorused Billy and Ellen.

"I better not," said Betty Jane.

"We're going to have lots of things to eat, aren't we?" said Linda, who had fallen down in the wagon and already had hay in her hair.

"Yes," said Betty Jane, throwing a handful of hay at Eddie, who was sitting opposite her. Before very long all of them had hay in their hair.

The wagon rattled along the road, past big fields where the cornstalks, whitish-brown, stood waiting to be cut down. Some fields were already cleared and the corn shocks stood in neat rows. Here an occasional pumpkin showed bright orange on the dull ground. The children sang as they rode along, but their eyes kept wandering over to the box that was between Betty Jane's knees.

In about three quarters of an hour the horses stopped beside a beautiful picnic ground. It was on the edge of a wood, with a view of a wide valley. There were long wooden tables with benches, and there were stone fire-places with ovens. It was such a lovely picnic spot that the children didn't mind getting out of the hay wagon.

As soon as Betty Jane got down she cried, "Oh, the ground is very damp!" She ran to the nearest table and placed her box on the end of it. When the children saw that Betty Jane was about to untie the string on the box, they all rushed to the table.

"Here! Let me help you," said Billy.

"Oh, dear," said Betty Jane, "the string is in a knot."

"I can get it out," cried Eddie. "I'm good at knots."

"I'll get a knife," said Christopher. He ran to Mr. Jackson, calling, "Can I have a knife, please?" In a moment he was back with the knife. "Here!" he said. "Here's a knife. Let me cut it." Everyone made way for Christopher. He put the knife blade under the string and sawed on it. Nothing happened.

"It's dull," cried Billy. "The knife is too dull."

Eddie ran to the farmer, who was unhitching the horses from the hay wagon. "Mister!" Eddie called. "Do you have a penknife?" The farmer reached into his pocket and pulled out a big one. "Oh, that's great!" said Eddie. "Thanks! I just want to cut the string on a box of candy."

"See that you bring it right back," said the farmer. "I'm taking the horses over to the pasture across the way. I'll be right back. Take good care of that knife and don't cut yourself."

"I will. I mean, I won't cut myself," said Eddie. "And I'll get you a piece of salt-water taffy." Eddie ran back to the group of children. "I've got a penknife," he shouted. He bent his head over the knife and pulled at one of the blades with his fingers. "Ouch! I broke my fingernail," he said. He pulled again. He couldn't open the blade.

"Here!" said his brother Joe. "Let me open it."

Eddie handed the knife to Joe. Joe pulled at the blade, but he couldn't open it either. "Take it to Father," said Betsy. "He can open it."

Joe took it to Betsy's father while the children took turns at trying to undo the knot in the string.

Betty Jane looked down at the ground and said, "I hope my feet aren't getting wet. My mother doesn't like it when I get my feet wet." No one paid any attention to Betty Jane's feet. They were only interested in Betty Jane's box.

Joe came back with the knife. It was open and the blade shone like fire as the sunlight struck it. "Stand back, everybody!" Joe cried. "This blade is sharp." The children gave Joe plenty of room as he stepped up to the box. One quick stroke of the knife, and the string was cut.

"Oh, thank you," said Betty Jane. Then, as everyone pressed around her, she lifted the lid of the box. There in the box lay Betty Jane's brown rubbers. The toes were turned up and there was a little bit of dried mud on one of them.

"Rubbers!" cried Billy.

"Rubbers!" Eddie groaned.

"Where's my knife?" said the farmer, walking up to Eddie.

"Oh, here it is," said Eddie, handing the knife to the farmer. "It wasn't salt-water taffy. It was rubbers."

"Can you imagine that?" said Joe to his twin. "Rubbers!"

Betty Jane was left alone to put on her rubbers. Soon

the children had forgotten their disappointment over the salt-water taffy, because they were all busy roasting hot dogs over glowing red embers. In no time, they drank up all the cocoa and ate all the baked beans. There wasn't a crumb of cake left when they packed up for the return trip, and they ate crunchy apples all the way home.

After the hay ride was over and Betsy reached home, she looked out of the living-room window. She looked across the garden to the summerhouse. A great big red harvest moon, hanging low in the sky, shone through the summerhouse and seemed to fill it.

"Oh, Father," Betsy cried, "come look at the moon in the summerhouse!"

Father came and stood beside Betsy. "I'm glad I built that summerhouse," he said, "if only to see that moon shining through it."

"It's a lovely summerhouse," said Betsy, a little sadly. "We had fun in it all summer. Now I guess it will get full of snow."

"No," said her father. "I'm going to board it up next week."

"Oh, dear!" sighed Betsy. "It won't look very pretty with old boards all over it, will it?"

"I'm going to paint them the color of that moon," said Father, "that beautiful orange-red. Then we'll hang evergreens around the top and it will look like a Christmas package."

"Oh, Father!" exclaimed Betsy. "Now I can't wait to see it in the snow!"

Betsy and her father stood at the window a long time. They watched the moon gradually rise out of the summerhouse. As it rose higher in the sky it grew smaller and turned from red to orange.

At last Betsy turned away from the window and walked over to the fire that was burning in the fireplace. She watched the flames dancing and listened to the wood crackling. "Winter is nice too," said Betsy. "Nice and cozy!"